"Won't you my mistress, Christabel?"

Alex's hand slid up her thigh. He watched as color seeped from her skin at the intimate caress.

It was a punishment. This, he was telling her, is the sort of woman you are, open to any man's touch. And the horror of it was that he was wrong; only he could unlock the passions of her body.

She closed her eyes, repelled by his calculating effrontery.

"I'm not cut out to be a plaything, Alex. Sorry, but that's the way it is."

"Oh, but you have an enormous talent for sex," he said insolently. "If a life without work bores you, you could always keep on modeling. Provided you're in my bed when I want you, of course."

"Sorry," she said again, because that was all she could trust herself to say, then turned and walked back down onto the beach....

Books by Robyn Donald

HARLEQUIN PRESENTS

HARLEQUIN ROMANCES

These books may be available at your local bookseller.

For a free catalog listing all titles currently available,
send your name and address to:

Harlequin Reader Service
P.O. Box 52040, Phoenix, AZ 85072-9988
Canadian address: Stratford, Ontario N5A 6W2

ROBYN DONALD

the gates of rangitatau

Harlequin Books

TORONTO • NEW YORK • LONDON
AMSTERDAM • PARIS • SYDNEY • HAMBURG
STOCKHOLM • ATHENS • TOKYO • MILAN

To
TAMSIN
with love

———————◆━━◆━◆———————

Harlequin Presents first edition February 1984
ISBN 0-373-10665-3

Original hardcover edition published in 1983
by Mills & Boon Limited

CHAPTER ONE

LIKE most models, Christabel Evans wasn't classically beautiful.

What she had that ensured her success was superb skin, sultry eyes of a shade between blue and green, and the kind of bone structure which enhanced any clothes she wore. So much so that designers often asked for her and photographers knew that almost every shot taken of her would be usable.

'What that means,' she told her closest friend, 'is that I'm totally forgettable. All you notice is the clothes!'

'Oh, you're an impossible cynic! I mean, you must know that that's not so.' Sarah eyed her closely. 'I'd kill for your cheekbones. And you have enormous eyes, and the longest, darkest lashes I've ever lusted after, skin like pale silk——'

'The rest is artificial,' Christabel interrupted, slight colour heating her cheeks. 'Fake. Under this skilfully applied red colouring my hair is mouse-brown, and you know yourself that anything can be done with cosmetics.'

Sarah, who did indeed know this, having been taught several very useful tricks by her friend, nevertheless stuck to her guns. 'You look good over breakfast,' she argued. 'Oh, not the exquisite creature who smiles and pouts out from the pages of the glossies, but actually I prefer your morning face. And I'll bet that whatever colour you used on your hair you'd look the same.'

Christabel eyed her up and down, grinning. 'How good you are for my ego! But the way I look over the breakfast table is irrelevant, at the moment, anyway. I mean—you're the one who's going to have to face the love of your life there in a few days. How does it feel to be an almost married lady?'

'Terrifying!' But Sarah didn't look terrified or anything but radiantly, gloriously happy. 'Oh, Chris, I'm so excited I can barely sleep! When I think that it's only a week before Ian and I are together and nothing will ever separate us again—well, I get a funny feeling in my toes.'

'In your *toes*?' Christabel pretended to be overcome with astonishment before both girls collapsed in schoolgirl giggles. After a while she said affectionately, 'Well, I guess Ian will soon change the location of that funny feeling. He deserves you, and you deserve him. I'll bet no one in Brisbane—no, in all *Australia*—has been wooed so ardently and with such romantic fervour.'

'Unless it's you—by Greg Bardsley,' Sarah retorted slyly.

For a moment Christabel looked much younger, vulnerable and unsure.

'Well—yes, we'll see,' was all that she said, but Sarah's eyebrows drew together in a slight frown.

Hurrying into speech to hide her unease, she asked, 'You're going out with him tonight, aren't you?'

'Yes.' With the unstudied grace which she had never appreciated Christabel picked up bag and wrap and cast a last, professional glance at herself in the mirror before giving an elaborate parody of a mannequin's twirl. 'O.K.?'

'Oh, very much so.' Sarah thought she had never seen her look better. Beneath the cool cynicism of the façade Christabel showed the world she was sensitive. And she was very much in love with Greg Bardsley.

Well, why not? Sarah asked herself as they exchanged goodbyes. O.K., so his family was socially prominent and he ambitious, but what better wife for a rising executive than a clever, sophisticated woman who had an enormous number of contacts in the world of the rich and the famous, whose charm was as natural as that fabulous skin and who would know exactly how to use those assets to help him? No snob herself, Sarah wasn't in the least concerned by her friend's undistinguished background.

The Bardsleys were one of the great pastoral families. To be sure, Greg's particular branch had fallen on hard times, but he had brains and the determination to bring the family business back to its former status. His mother and Sarah's were dearest friends; it was Sarah who, two months ago, had introduced him to Christabel. Ever since she had wondered at the faint dismay their instant rapport caused her.

Now, she stood frowning at the door as it closed behind Christabel's elegant figure until the sound of the telephone banished all other thoughts and with the splendid selfishness of those who love she flew across the room to answer it.

Christabel, meanwhile, took a taxi to a discreet door in a discreet façade and was welcomed into a discreet foyer by a discreet doorman.

'Mr Bardsley is already here, Miss Evans,' he told her, smiling slightly at the sudden radiance which his words brought to the fine-boned, patrician face.

Yes, there he was, an inch or so taller than her, so distinguished that her heart swelled as he took her hand in his for a brief moment before leading her to their table, small and private, tucked in behind a screen.

Once, early in their relationship, she had made the mistake of kissing his cheek when they met. Gently he had made it clear that those kisses, common coinage in her circle, were not for him. At the time his attitude had hurt, but closer knowledge of him had brought comprehension. Greg did not like casual endearments, meaningless caresses; his fastidious nature meant that in their public life he was oddly formal.

So different from those precious private moments they spent together ... !

Hot blood warmed her throat at the memory of one such night last week. A swift glance from beneath the thick lashes so envied by Sarah revealed that he too was remembering her passionate abandon, the sudden savage desire which had turned him from the self-contained man she knew to one driven by a hunger so fierce that had Sarah not come upon them there must have been only one end to the evening.

Something glittered in the depths of his eyes, but the firm mouth remained set in a smile, revealing nothing.

'How beautiful you are,' he said deep in his throat. 'How very beautiful, my own love.'

Only two months ago Christabel would have said, and believed it, that she could no longer blush. But Greg had the power to turn her blood to fire. Within his her hand trembled until it was released so that he could sit her down.

The food was superb, carefully chosen, brilliantly cooked and served. Like the other diners they paid it due homage with their most elegant clothes and a general air of restrained gaiety. Only the very wealthy and those whose knowledge of good cuisine led them to it came to this restaurant. The owner very carefully avoided the stigma of being fashionable; in a way it was like a club.

And it was as expensive as it was good. Christabel hid her concern. It was like Greg to want only the best, but although he had worked miracles with his business he was not yet in the category which could pay prices like this without blinking. And by now he must know that she would be completely happy to eat hamburgers with him in the rain.

'Everything ready for the big day?' he asked after he had dealt with the menu and wine list.

Christabel laughed. 'Almost. We're driving down to the Gold Coast tomorrow, taking the wedding dress with us. Sarah says we'll walk into a madhouse there! Her mother is a darling, but she panics.'

He looked at her over the rim of his glass, fine brows drawn together in a frown. 'I thought Sarah had already gone. And that you weren't going down until Friday.'

'Well, that was the original plan,' she said, astounded to hear a placatory note in her voice. 'But there was a delay with the wedding dress. Poor Sarah had to stay on for a final fitting today.' She smiled slowly at him. 'And as you're not going to be here and I've left this week clear of jobs so that I could help Sarah, I thought I'd go down with her. Instead of moping around waiting for you to come back from your dreary business trip.'

'I see,' he said after a moment's pause, then smiled and touched her hand lightly. 'Sensible of you, darling. I'd rather you were there than here without me.'

She laughed, a warm pleased little sound. 'I'm more than capable of looking after myself,' she retorted, but his attitude thrilled her. It was so many years since anyone had been protective towards her; her mother, that practical woman who had seen that her daughter's particular assets were marketable, encouraging, almost forcing her to exploit them from the age of sixteen, had been sensible and tough-minded. She had ensured that her daughter could cope with any situation, giving her hard, unsentimental advice on men and morals. In her way she had been good for Christabel, strongly squashing any tendencies towards the starry-eyed idealism which would have been so dangerous to a girl whose looks made her automatic prey for the opposite sex. Unfortunately, Brenda Evans' crisp lack of warmth had had the effect of building in her daughter a hard, glossy exterior which fooled all but those few perceptive enough to seek out the warmth and shyness hidden beneath. As a protection it was very effective, but life behind it was lonely.

Correction. Had been lonely, until Greg came along with his grave courtesy and his intuitive recognition of her needs. Not since she had been taken from her home and father ten years ago, a frightened twelve-year-old, had she felt so cherished and understood.

'Oh, you've made a very good job of looking after yourself.' He lifted his glass in a silent toast, adding after he had drunk, 'But you need someone to care for you, Chris. You're far too beautiful to be alone in a world full of wolves.'

For a moment her heart stopped. Surely this was not a proposal—not here, not now!

But no, of course not. Greg smiled at her and made some other remark and her heart began to beat again, irregularly but with increasing speed.

Had those few words been a sort of prelude? Or were they just the kind of light compliment men felt impelled to make when dining with a reasonably attractive woman? Not Greg, though. She drew some comfort from the fact that he rarely said anything unless he meant it. He paid her the supreme compliment of thoughtfulness.

Christabel was no longer bitter that many men saw her as nothing more than a body and a face. Her mother's choice of a career for her had made such a reaction almost inevitable. But her life as a model would be a short one; when it was over she intended to go to university and take law. Since she had first started earning she had saved for that eventuality.

Only marriage would sway her from her purpose. Sometimes she hoped that her husband would enjoy the idea of a wife who was a lawyer. But as the years passed her ideals crumbled beneath the hard reality of men's actions and attitudes. It was as her mother warned her. Although there were plenty of men prepared to swear their love in return for rights to her body, none of them intended more than a sensual exploitation, a cynical ownership without respect or even liking.

At first she had expected Greg to be the same. Her liking had been immediate and incandescent, but during their first dates she had waited with sick certainty for him to make the inevitable proposition.

To her astonishment, an astonishment which revealed just how suspicious she had become, he made no effort to coax her into his bed. From the first he had treated her with consideration, talked to her as if she was an intelligent human being, made no move without ascertaining that his touch was pleasing to her, that she liked the light kisses he gave her, the feel of his skin against hers.

So she had fallen in love with an incredulous fervour which was intensified by the long years of repression, her hungry heart clamouring for the comfort she had believed denied to her for ever.

The years of caution prevented her from revealing that love until a few nights ago, when passion had lowered her guard to disclose the ardent woman he had made her.

Now she thought, he *must* know how I feel about him, shyness clotting her throat as she glanced across at him.

But he was not looking at her. Her eyes had focused on a point above and behond her head and he was frowning, his head slightly turned as he listened.

'*Damn*!' he swore softly, his rueful gaze moving back to her face. 'Sorry, darling, but that subdued commotion down there is one of my rather important clients. He's just come in and he's going to see me any minute.'

'Is that a disaster?'

He must have divined her withdrawal, for he touched her hand in swift reassurance. 'He looks as though he's been drinking and I don't want to expose you to his crassness. You wouldn't like the way he behaves. He's a boor when he's had a few too many.' His mouth tightened as he finished drily, 'Unfortunately, he's important to me. Would you mind very much if I went over now to take the war to the enemy's camp? He's not likely to interrupt us if I do that.'

'Of course I don't mind.'

'Bless you!'

A tender smile shaped Christabel's lips as he rose. Darling Greg, so gallant! For a moment a bleak, lost emptiness darkened her expression as she recalled a few incidents in the past when she'd had to repel intimacies far worse than anything Greg's client could produce in a place like this. Still, she'd survived, and relatively unscathed.

Her long fingers, unadorned except by the rosy polish on her nails, curved around the stem of the wineglass. Within it the wine gleamed, pale, straw-coloured, dry yet with the flavour and tang of grape imprisoned in it. Suddenly thirsty, she picked up the glass and sipped its contents.

Some compulsion stronger than her will dragged her eyes upwards from their contemplation of the goblet. At the far end of the room a man had stood up, clearly on his way out. He had dined alone and he was looking at her, eyes glinting beneath straight, slanted brows which gave him the look of a satyr. Tall, big in his conventional dinner jacket yet more elegant than any other man she had ever seen, he was dark, dark-skinned, dark-eyed, his dark hair afire with tawny lights in the subdued glow of the lamps. Strong bones had tanned skin stretched over them; his brow was broad and cheekbones high and prominent, but the most noticeable feature in an inordinately handsome face was a jaw and chin of such determination that Christabel felt overwhelmed by an impression of stark, uncompromising strength.

The dark survey ran with electric precision over the smooth pallor of her shoulders and arms. He was not even trying to hide the sensual pleasure her body gave him.

Her skin tightened in the age-old signal of danger and she felt a boost of adrenalin in her bloodstream. For a long, long moment their glances locked, before, as if he recognised her reaction he smiled, a brief, knowing

movement of beautifully formed lips, then turned away
in a swirl of deferential waiters.

As he walked past Christabel kept her face averted
and her lashes lowered, but she felt the impact of his
glance for minutes afterwards. Whoever he was, and he
was clearly someone, he packed a lethal charge, like a
bolt of dark lightning.

When Greg returned, apologetic yet with an
undertone of some nameless emotion in his voice, she
had finished her wine and was well on the way to
regaining the composure which had been stripped from
her by that brief, unnerving little incident.

'Let's go,' Greg said abruptly an hour or so later.
'You don't want to dance, do you, darling?'

'No.' It was still quite early and normally she loved
being in his arms, but somehow the night had lost its
glamour. And as Sarah had threatened to leave at some
appalling hour the next morning, it was sensible to get
home early.

She said as much, and Greg, as he tucked her
tenderly into the car, commented, 'Me, too, I'm afraid.
I wonder why they send flights off at such incredible
times. Seven o'clock, would you believe?'

'Poor darling.' She sighed, her spirits oppressed by
the knowledge that she wouldn't be seeing him for three
days. 'Not that I think we'll be leaving that early. I'm
sure I heard the phone go as I left, which almost
certainly means Ian is back. If it was him they'll be at
the Maidstones' party.'

Back at the empty flat she wondered fleetingly if she
had been sensible telling Greg to all intents and
purposes that they had the place to themselves for
hours yet, but when he drew her into his arms she went
willingly, warmed and made secure by his lovemaking.
Trembling, she abandoned her defences to the hot
current of desire. Against her throat he whispered her
name and she groaned, not protesting as his hand
touched and cupped the small thrusting peak of her

breast. Her body tensed and then she moved convulsively against him, instinct with the need to lose herself in the driving force of his masculinity.

Until the click of the lock in the front door jerked them apart, flushed and frustrated.

Beneath his breath Greg swore, soft vicious syllables abruptly cut off as Sarah came in, a Sarah strangely bright-eyed, her pretty face set in uncharacteristically stern lines.

'Sorry,' she said curtly, not looking at either of them. 'Chris, can you come with me, please?'

'What is it?' In the bedroom Christabel stared at her, her hand at her heart as she saw the strain, the anguish in her friend's expression. 'Sarah—it's not *Ian*! Is it? *Sarah!*'

'*No!*' Sarah flung her arms around Christabel, holding her close as she said in a quick, goaded voice, 'I've spent an hour trying to think of ways to break it gently, but there are no ways. Ian told me when we— he's just come back from Melbourne and he saw Fliss Thomassin there, he's known her for years and he said—oh, Chris, it's Greg! He's engaged to her. To Fliss. It's all signed and settled. They're going to announce it in a month's time, on her birthday. Oh, Chris, I'm so sorry. But I had to tell you.'

The frightened, rapid words stopped as Christabel disengaged herself. She said nothing, did not even look at Sarah as she walked with her gliding, model-girl's gait back into the sitting room.

'Chris?'

In tones harsh with self-control she told him of Sarah's accusation, watching with the hard, suspicious eyes of a woman threatened. And knew the truth of it before he admitted it, his arrogant head held high, no sign of shame or remorse in his expression.

'I have to,' he said angrily. 'It's the only way I can get Alex Thomassin's support.'

'But why?' This could not be her, this woman of ice, her voice cool as a mountain stream.

'Because without it, my dear, the business I've worked so hard to put back on its feet is going to go straight down the drain. And that is not going to happen, not if there's any way I can prevent it.'

'Including marrying a woman you don't love?'

He shrugged, his eyes never wavering from her face. 'Oh, don't feel sorry for Fliss. She knows exactly what she's getting. This is not her first marriage.'

'I hope you'll both be happy,' she said, pride holding her head high.

Greg smiled. 'As happy as it's in us to be,' he returned. 'Fliss will have a husband and children, that's all she wants, and I'll have big brother Alex's money and acumen to help put my business on its feet and——' his voice dropped several tones as he came towards her and pulled her into his arms, '—a kind, sensual lover to keep my heart young.'

His mouth forced hers open; the heat of his desire enveloped her, melting the icy shock into a torrent of need and hunger. And as tears filled her eyes she responded, because she loved him.

'Oh, God,' he whispered brokenly a long time later, 'Don't make it any harder for me than it is, my darling, my love. At least give me credit for loving you.'

He meant it. Christabel closed her eyes, anguish tearing at her heart with its cruel claws. As much as he could need anyone he needed her, but his desire for power and wealth was greater than any emotion she could rouse in him. She had thought him determined and been proud of it; now, too late, she saw the strength of his determination and it was ruthlessness.

'I think you'd better go,' she said, keeping such a tight rein on her voice that the words came out in a flat monotone.

Slowly, his eyes never leaving hers, his hands came up to cup her face, their tremor transmitted through skin and bone to her.

'Why the hell couldn't Sarah have gone home when

she was supposed to!' he exclaimed thickly. 'I'd planned—I'd hoped that tonight I'd make you mine.'

He must have felt her flinch away from him, for his voice, harsh with emotion, faltered as he muttered, 'But it's inevitable, my lovely Christabel, because you love me, and beneath that cool composed façade there's a passionate woman. Look at me, my darling.'

Slowly, forced by his insistence, her lashes lifted. And he smiled, and bent his head and took her mouth again. But when his hand slid up to cup her breast she shuddered and broke away from him, and he let her go, failing to hide his satisfaction at her ardent response.

'I'll go now,' he said after a moment. 'I'm sorry that you had to hear so unkindly——'

'Is there a *kind* way of telling such news?' she asked hoarsely.

He frowned but refrained from coming any closer. 'No, but at least I could have held you and comforted you while I told you,' he said. 'You're in shock now, but when you've got over it you'll see that in lots of ways we'll have the sweets of love without any of the bitterness. Just remember, Christabel, that I love you more than I've ever loved any other woman.'

Sarah came in when she heard the outer door click behind him and stood looking at Christabel, her features rigid with control. One glance at her friend's averted face brought hot tears to her eyes.

'Tell me to go to bed if you want to,' she said quietly. 'I know you prefer to lick your wounds in private, but if you want to talk, I'm available. Chris, I *had* to tell you.'

'Yes, of course.' It was a relief to sink into a chair, to kick off the elegant sandals she had donned with such high hopes, was it only a few hours before?

'I hated it but—oh, Chris, how could he?'

Christabel's deep, slow voice quickened. 'He said it need make no difference to us. I gather it's to be a merger rather than a marriage. Felicity Thomassin wants children and a husband and Greg wants her share of the Thomassin money. Or Alex Thomassin's backing.' She gave a twisted, cynical smile. 'Somehow I can't see myself as a mistress, but oh, Sarah, I don't think I'm going to be able to hold out against him. I love him so!'

Sarah swallowed, horrified by the raw desolation in the deep voice. Speaking briskly, she said, 'What you need is something hot and milky and sweet to drink and to hell with the calories.'

'Thank you.' Drained, taut with the effort of keeping control, Christabel leaned her head back against the chair, eyes closed, hands clenched as she fought an anguish so piercing that she thought she might die from its pain.

When Sarah reappeared with cocoa Christabel opened her eyes, staring at her as if she had never seen her before.

'Here.' Sarah proffered the mug. 'I know you don't like it, but it will help you sleep.'

For a few moments they sipped before Sarah asked hesitantly, 'Chris, would it be so bad? Oh, I know you're hurt—who wouldn't be?—but would it make so much of a difference to your life if you keep—if you— well, if you let things go on as they are?'

Drums seemed to be beating in Christabel's temples, thumping so hard and so painfully that she could no longer think straight. 'He doesn't want things to go on as they are,' she retorted flatly, pressing her palms to her head. 'He wants me to be his mistress. To sleep with him!'

'Oh!' Sarah was nonplussed, and to hide it gulped a mouthful of cocoa, choked and spluttered.

Christabel began to laugh, recognised in time the note of hysteria and forced herself to stop. 'You might well say oh! I haven't—we haven't made love.'

'Oh,' poor Sarah said again, inadequately. 'I'm sorry, It's just that——'

Christabel eased her throbbing head back on to the

chair, turning her face so that the leather cooled one burning cheek.

'I know,' she said flatly. 'That time you came back early—and tonight. You have every reason for assuming that we were lovers. My God, how *dare* he! C-court another woman for her money and expect me to—to make him welcome! I could kill him!' She pushed the backs of her hands against her eyes, weeping in real earnest now. 'But I think—I don't know if I can resist him. I hate him—but I want him so!'

'Oh, Chris, don't cry, he's not worth it.' Sarah jumped to her feet and perched herself on the arm of the chair beside Christabel, hugging her for a moment with all of the fierce protectiveness of a mother with her only child. 'Darling, *don't*, please. He's a swine, an absolute swine, and you're worth a thousand of him.'

Christabel took a deep breath, held it for seconds before expelling it. 'Oh, how true,' she said with dry bitterness, 'but it doesn't help matters, does it?'

'Just keep his general beastliness firmly in mind and you'll be too angry to feel so miserable,' Sarah told her wisely, bestowing a further quick hug before returning to her own chair.

Cocoa was imbibed in silence for more minutes until Sarah asked tentatively, 'Chris, tell me to go to hell if you like, but have you ever made love with anyone?'

'No.' She met the younger girl's gaze with a faint hint of defiance. 'There are plenty of twenty-two-year-old virgins around, you know, we just don't advertise our existence.'

'And you're sure you don't want to——?'

'No!' Christabel drew a deep, painful breath, striving for calmness. 'I love Greg. I don't think I'll ever love anyone else. But my mother was a very moral lady and before she died she instilled a whole set of very Puritan ethics in me. Sex belongs to marriage, that sort of thing.' Dropping her wryly frivolous air, she continued in anguished desperation, 'He can't love me or he would never have suggested such a degrading scheme. He—there's no way he can respect me, Sarah, he's totally confident that as soon as I get over the initial shock I'll agree to his plan. That's what hurts so. I love him and he says he loves me, but he doesn't. He never has. It was all lies, everything he's said.'

'Did he promise you marriage?'

'No,' she returned forlornly. 'Stupid, thick idiot that I am, I just hoped for it. I should have known that men like Greg don't marry little models from nowhere. They just sleep with them.'

'Rubbish!' Sarah objected trenchantly. 'He's a beast and you're a lady. I wish I wasn't getting married so soon and leaving you to cope alone.' A sudden thought made her wince. 'Oh God, he'll be at the wedding. And so will she—Felicity Thomassin, I mean. The Thomassins are friends of the parents. It was quite a feather in Mum's cap when both she and Alex agreed to come.' She stared at her friend in horror. 'Oh, Chris, let's hope he doesn't come!'

'He'll be there,' Christabel said with bleak conviction, knowing the truth of what she said. 'If only to make sure I don't queer his pitch by telling all to his fiancée.'

'What will we do?'

'*You* will marry Ian and be perfectly happy, as you were meant to be,' Christabel told her firmly, draining the last of the cocoa with a grimace. 'And I shall behave perfectly all day—models have to be quite competent actresses, you know. And then I'll go home. No one will ever find me there.'

Sarah's mouth dropped open a moment. 'Home? You mean back to——? But, Chris—it will mean giving up everything you've worked so hard for!'

Christabel's haunted eyes closed in momentary blindness. 'Tonight, after he'd admitted that he was marrying her, he kissed me and I—and I responded like a bride on her wedding night. I go up in flames for him, and he knows it. I am *not* going to wait around like a sitting duck! And I've just had a letter from my father. Reading between the lines I'm certain that he and my stepmother could do with my help.'

'I'd sleep on it,' Sarah suggested tentatively. 'You'll almost certainly feel better in the morning.'

But the morning only reinforced that sudden decision. As Sarah drove down towards Surfers Paradise, that bustling, frenetic playground of Australia, Christabel's determination hardened into resolution. It had been so long since she had been home, so many years when her only contact with her father had been their weekly letters. Why, she had not even met her stepmother, although she knew the gentle, kind features from photographs. Home! Perhaps there she could forget Greg's betrayal.

Ten years ago her mother had left her husband, making for Brisbane and a new life, as far away as her bank balance allowed from the remote farm where she had spent the previous thirteen years. Christabel had written to her father, spent holidays back with him and missed everything about her home until six years ago when Donald had married again. Her mother had suggested that she give him and his new wife time to settle down together, and since then she had not gone back. Why, she had a small three-year-old brother called Scott whom she had never seen.

Now Elaine was pregnant again, making heavy weather of it this time.

Perhaps it was fate of a sort that Christabel should feel the need of the solid physical presence of the father she had adored, just when it seemed that he needed her.

As soon as they arrived at Surfers Paradise she organised her journey home.

'But why the very next day after the wedding?' Sarah wailed. 'Why not stay until Ian and I get back?'

'No.' The decision made, she was firm. 'I'll go home to the flat as soon as you leave for your honeymoon. It will be better that way.' Unspoken was her acceptance of the fact that Greg would be at the wedding. 'Your mother has very kindly arranged a ride back for me.'

'Yes, with the Blakes, who always leave every party so they can be in bed at ten-thirty,' grumbled Sarah. 'Oh, I suppose it's for the best, but I'm going to miss you so!'

'Nonsense. You'll have Ian, and he's all that you'll need from now on.'

'A woman can't have too many good female friends,' Sarah told her with one of her quick flashes of wisdom.

'I'll write, I promise, every week. Mind you, I'll expect answers! Just don't give anyone my address.'

And with that Sarah had to be content. Indeed the following few days were so hectic that there was no time for other confidences, no time for anything but frantic last-minute organising. No time to lie on the superb beach, no time to explore the shops, not even time to watch the pelicans and ibises as they went about their avian business on the lawn, solemn and purposeful. Sarah's parents owned a house facing one of the canals which are so much a feature of Surfers. It was a beautiful, modern, exquisitely decorated house with a large cruiser moored a few yards away and a garden where hibiscuses and African tulip trees bloomed.

From the moment they arrived the house seemed full of people, relatives, friends, caterers, and in the bustle and the constant entertaining Christabel barely had time to think. So determined was she that nothing was to spoil Sarah's wedding day that she knocked herself out each night with sleeping pills. Between the drugs and the activity she gave every appearance of being her usual self, tall, perfectly groomed and mannered, an asset to any occasion. And if anyone saw through the flat opacity of her gaze to the aching desolation beneath no one remarked on it.

CHAPTER TWO

THE wedding was delightful.

Everyone said so. Sarah made a charming, ecstatic bride and Ian was everything that a bridegroom is supposed to be, proud and tender and possessive and nervous. The bridesmaids were enchanting, Christabel and four little nieces who, miracle of miracles, all behaved with the utmost circumspection. The best man was helpful and made a witty speech at the reception, looking as if he couldn't believe his luck at being partnered by such a beautiful bridesmaid.

Of course there were the usual panics, but by eight o'clock in the evening all that was forgotten and things were going with a swing. And Christabel, smiling, poised and gay, thought that if help didn't come to her soon she would embarrass everyone by weeping bitterly in front of them all.

For Greg and Felicity Thomassin had been together all day, she with a bell of deep mahogany hair and a beautiful, proud face, he with his usual air of well-groomed self-confidence.

And Christabel discovered what it was like to bleed slowly to death inside, to die so silently that no one knew.

'Oh—*God*!' she breathed, turning her head away from the picture they made as they danced together.

'What was that?' Sarah's mother looked startled. She hadn't heard what Christabel had said, but as she followed the direction of her blind gaze a smile creased the kindly, beautifully made up face. 'Oh yes, I see who you mean, my dear. That's Alex Thomassin. Come and be—ah, trust him to pick out the prettiest girl in the room! He's a devil, that one, but so handsome you have

24

to forgive him anything! Alex, my dear, this is Christabel Evans.' She made the introduction in a clear, precise voice with an undercurrent of laughter, for the two were staring at each other as though they had just that moment fallen in love.

He was the man who had stripped her so assessingly across the restaurant the night she had learned of Greg's perfidy. Desperately she searched his face to see if there was any recognition in the eyes, dark as slate, which roved her face. And almost sighed her relief when the only thing reflected in the handsome features was a kind of stunned appreciation mixed with mockery. Apart from colouring, the dark red hair and the tanned skin, he didn't resemble his sister at all, unless it was in the proud hauteur of features and that insolent jut of jaw she had noticed immediately. Where Felicity was small and slight he towered over Christabel, herself taller than average, with wide shoulders and an animal litheness which even faultlessly tailored clothes could not hide.

Instead of shaking the hand she extended he took it to his lips and pressed a kiss on the throbbing vein at the wrist, holding her eyes until a faint colour touched her skin and she looked away.

'I've heard a lot about you,' he said in a voice that matched the rest of him. Deep and dangerous.

Christabel's lashes flew up as she registered that he was angry.

'Unfortunately I know only your name,' she riposted sweetly, feeling a subtle quickening in her blood.

Someone, somewhere, had turned the music down. Together they stood in a little bubble of silence, her hand lost in his long-fingered grasp while around them the party roared.

'Then I'll have to fill you in on a few details,' he drawled, and drew her into his arms, his expression enigmatic as he stared down into the face lifted to his.

Christabel was accustomed to being stared at.

Training had taught her the best way to make use of her assets, the enormous, slightly tilted eyes with their unusual colour and the high stark cheekbones which photographed so well. And her body, of course, slender and sinuous, naturally graceful with long fragile bones and pale satin skin. There were thousands of women in Australia far better-looking; it was her good luck that she was tall and photographed like a dream.

Yet Alex Thomassin said quietly, 'How incredibly lovely you are,' and the bold glitter of his gaze told her that he meant it.

Christabel turned her head away, cursing as tell-tale heat crawled across her cheekbones. Just as if she was a seventeen-year-old at her first ball instead of a woman whose heart and life were lying in shattered fragments at her feet.

'Christabel,' he said, and when, startled, she looked up, he smiled and quoted, '"*The lovely lady, Christabel*"—it's from a poem by Coleridge. Have you a romantic mother?'

'No,' she returned bluntly. Far from it. Her mother had realised what assets those eyes and cheekbones, that body were, and had set *her* daughter's feet on the path to modelling.

'Really? Is it your real name? Or an agent's invention?'

Reluctantly she smiled. 'My real name.'

Her eyes, roving the room to escape the too-intimate gaze of her partner, were caught by Greg's. The familiar pang of pain and desire clutched deep in her stomach. Deliberately she lifted her gaze and smiled again at Alex Thomassin, slowly, seductively.

'Dreadful, isn't it,' she said. 'At least, it sticks in the mind. Once it's been learnt no one ever forgets it.'

A swift glance slanted from beneath her lashes showed Greg's lips tightened in anger, his face white beneath the tan. Serves him right, the swine! she thought exultantly. Let him think that she and Alex

Thomassin were enjoying each other's company. A kind of desperate recklessness brought a sparkle of defiance to her eyes. Willing herself to relax, she felt her partner respond to her invitation by gathering her closer to his lean length.

Above her ear his voice was amused. 'And it's important for your name to stick in the mind?'

'In my job, yes.'

'Do you like being a model?'

Her shoulders, smooth and seductive above silk, lifted slightly. 'It's hard work, but it has its moments.' And she told him some of those moments, making him laugh at the incredible vanity of a photographer, an incident involving an extremely aggressive emu which took an instant dislike to her, and a riotous fashion parade when for a while it seemed that only an act of God would be enough to get the compère sufficiently sober to do her job.

Laughing, he was very attractive, the dark perilous charm overlaid with humour. And he made her laugh, too, to her considerable surprise.

But while she was talking to him and while they danced, her head tipped back to reveal the lovely inviting arc of her throat, she was watching that bleak look on Greg's face intensify into barely hidden fury. And the recklessness inside her expanded and grew. For the first time since Sarah's bombshell had exploded over her world she felt alive again.

Alex Thomassin must have got his duty dances over and done with early on, for from then on he danced only with her. When the music stopped he summoned champagne and watched, smiling, as she drank it. Rakishly handsome, those straight brows lifted in quizzical interest, he carried himself with the kind of inbuilt authority which had head waiters thoroughly intimidated. He was as sexy as hell, and for tonight he was Christabel's lifeline.

When it was time for Sarah and Ian to go Christabel

ran up the stairs to offer her help and Sarah hissed, 'There, what did I tell you? Better fish in the sea and all that jazz! Just be careful, Chris love. Ian might be a barracuda, but Alex is a shark, swift and deadly.'

Buoyed by the pleasant rashness engendered by champagne, Christabel laughed. 'Oh, don't worry about me, I'm not stupid enough to get tangled up with that one.'

'Well—no, only he's definitely——' but then her mother came in and whatever Sarah had been going to say was lost in farewells and kisses and a few tears.

When at last they had gone, showered with confetti and rice and rose petals, the party might have died except that everyone was determined to keep it going.

Everyone except Christabel. The rush of bubbles in her blood had died and although the recklessness remained it had become transmuted into a hard bitter emotion which shadowed the depths of her eyes. She stood aloof from the laughing noisy crowd, the light glittering on her red head as she twisted it, looking for the Blakes who were to take her to Brisbane and who, surely, must be ready by now to go.

Cruel fingers caught her wrist, tightening on the slender bones as she automatically tried to jerk free.

'Oh, no,' Greg bit out savagely, hauling her into a small alcove where they were partly hidden. 'You're not getting away so easily! Just what the hell do you think you're playing at, you stupid little fool? Alex Thomassin has every intention of taking you to bed with him tonight!'

The raw jealousy in his tones pleased her. 'And perhaps,' she spat, 'I have every intention of letting him!'

His fingers on her wrist tightened unbearably. 'You bitch!' he ground out harshly. 'My God, I could——'

'Christabel?'

They stood staring at each other, Christabel's head flung back in defiance, Greg with a white line around his mouth, pale eyes blazing.

Then she twisted free, said loudly, 'Coming, Alex,' and left without a backward glance, a wild, exultant pulse beating through her body, forcing the blood through her veins and up in a high surge of colour across her face. An old Bible text came to her mind. *"Vengeance is mine, saith the Lord,"* but tonight vengeance was Christabel's, and oh, it was sweet!

Not far from the alcove Alex was leaning against the wall, a glass of champagne in each hand. He straightened as he saw her and smiled, handing her one of them.

'I thought I heard your voice,' he said coolly, heavy lids lowered over dark grey eyes. 'Who were you with?'

'No one of any importance.'

Just for a moment she felt the impact of his gaze, dagger-sharp, and shivered.

'You look hot,' he said quietly. 'Drink your champagne.'

The rest of the evening blurred into a parade of music and dancing, laughter and champagne, the comforting strength of Alex's arm around her and the dark glitter of appreciation in his eyes whenever they rested on her. Occasionally she saw Greg, always with his fiancée, but only once did her eyes meet his and then she rejoiced at the frustration and fury she saw there. Why should she be the only one to suffer? Let him think that tonight she and Alex Thomassin would lie together in rapturous ecstasy, that she would give this stranger what she had withheld from him!

Towards midnight the Blakes came up to her, smiling, obviously ready to go.

'Why not let me drive you?' Alex suggested smoothly. 'I'm going up to Brisbane after this.'

Just for a moment Christabel hesitated, Greg's warning ominous in her ears. Then she laughed and said, 'I'd like that.'

So the Blakes left and Alex asked, 'Where do you live?'

She gave him the name of the street and he nodded and said, 'Tell me when you want to go.'

'Not for hours yet,' she laughed, and tilted her head back to look up at him from beneath her lashes, deliberately flirtatious.

The hard mouth smiled and he bent his head and kissed her, sensuously, so swiftly that for a moment she thought she must have imagined it.

'Do you often do that?' she asked, smiling in her turn and thinking, no more champagne!

'No, but you're very beautiful. A temptation to even the most conventional of men.'

'And you're very bold.' Above his shoulder she met the impotent jealousy of Greg's glance and turned her head and rested it against the width of Alex's chest.

'Tired?'

'I must be.'

A lean finger lifted her chin; her face was subjected to the keen question of his eyes.

'Then let's go,' he said after a moment.

So they went, away through the warm, eucalyptus-scented night in a fabulously comfortable Rolls. For a while as they drove through the razzle of Surfers they talked, lightly, of things of little importance, but before long the intensity of her emotions combined with the wine and her head drooped, nodded and slipped sideways to rest on a hard shoulder.

Her name, repeated twice, woke her. She could hear Alex, hear the amusement in the deep tones, but she couldn't open her eyes.

'Come on, sweetheart,' he said, then laughed softly and picked her up.

'Careful,' she yawned. 'I'm not as light as I look.'

'Ah, but I'm very strong.'

He was too, immensely strong, and the strength of those arms about her gave her a kind of security, but she stiffened, saying with great dignity, 'You can put me down.'

'Sure you can walk?'

This made her angry. Haughtily she opened her eyes and stared up at him; he was smiling, the strong bones prominent, the straight winged brows sharply accenting his face. He had long thick lashes, sooty black. They lay now almost on the tanned skin of his cheeks, but beneath them there glittered something, she decided hazily, that was—almost sinister. He was very big, very tough, very sure of himself—and of her.

'I can walk,' she said. Then she lost her stomach.

Of course they were in a lift, but she gulped and grabbed at him, and that smile reappeared and he bent his head and kissed her again. But this time it was no quick kiss. Slowly, with great enjoyment, he coaxed her lips to part beneath his, using what she dimly realised to be a very considerable expertise to persuade her into relaxing her guard.

Warning bells clanged fiercely in her ears. She stiffened, pulling away, her eyes widening to their furthest extent. As the elevator sighed to a halt he lifted his mouth and kissed each smooth half-moon of lid closed.

'Alex——' she began, belatedly realising how great her danger was.

'Sh,' he soothed. 'Shall I carry you?'

'No! I can walk!'

But again she was caught up in the hard strength of his arms. Head whirling, she clutched his shoulders trying to count up the number of drinks she had had. Not many, but for days she had eaten practically nothing. Now it was all catching up with her and she should have been terrified out of her mind, but instead she relaxed.

Something warm and soft met her cheek.

'Tired,' she said wistfully, curving into it.

'Very tired,' he agreed, a note of laughter in the dry tones. Hands lifted her legs, removed the high strappy sandals, then smoothed over the fine skin of her feet and ankles, lingering, stroking, strangely erotic.

Christabel flexed her legs, enjoying the sensual massage. She wore no stockings and the smooth caress brought a thousand subtle sensations into play.

'Now,' that amused voice said, 'what are we going to do about this pretty thing? It looks immensely crushable. Turn over, Christabel.'

It had the authentic ring of authority. Obediently she twisted on to her stomach, felt the fastenings loosen and allowed him to free her from the silken folds of her bridesmaid's dress. The bed was warm and smooth and comfortable. She wanted only to be left to sleep, to sleep in those safe arms which had held her so securely.

'Hmm. Very little in the way of underpinnings. It's lucky we're in the sub-tropics or you'd be in imminent danger of frostbite!'

Christabel smiled and stretched, turning over on to her side. One arm she pushed up the pillow, the other she lifted across her eyes to keep out the light. Uncomfortable, she turned on to her back, moving slowly and languorously.

In quite a different tone of voice Alex said, 'You're every bit as desirable as Aphrodite, my dear, and if you don't have too much of a hangover tomorrow morning I might just take you up on that invitation. However, for tonight——'

'Oh, shut up!' she interrupted, angry because he thought she was drunk and she wasn't, just very tired.

She opened her eyes, peeping at him from beneath the slender curve of her arm. He was standing beside the bed, his features sharpened with incredible restraint, dark eyes restlessly surveying the pale length of her body.

Wherever they rested Christabel felt a tiny impact, like an explosion of nerves. His desire was a tangible thing, dark, frightening, yet she was not frightened because although he wanted her his will was so strong that he would not take her. Not unless she made it clear that she desired him.

A pulse beat heavily in her ears. With a dry mouth she whispered, 'You—you talk too much.'

Surely there was nothing provocative in such a statement, even if she didn't know why she made it. But as if those few words had been an invitation he knelt beside the bed. His face loomed over her, dark, saturnine.

Very softly he said, 'Amazing how wrong first impressions can be. I thought you——'

Impelled by something she didn't recognise, she put up her hand and touched the warm hard line of his mouth.

'Hush,' she whispered in strange, thick tones. 'Please, don't. . . .'

She thought he was going to kiss her again, but the dark head swooped, his mouth opened on to her breast and she gasped, her body jerking in a spasm of something so powerful that she went under like a drowning person, her hands clenching on themselves as sensation, piercingly sweet, stabbed through her body.

'Gently, darling,' he said smoothly, his lips tormenting against the skin of her high young breasts. 'No wonder——'

She couldn't let him finish. Vaguely she knew that what he was about to say would hurt her. One hand touched the slightly rough skin of his cheek, holding his face between her breasts while the other slid beneath the silk of his shirt, delighting in the smooth skin beneath it. Heat scorched her. She knew that what she was inviting was wrong, she knew that she would wake in the morning bitterly regretting everything that was about to happen, but she could not have stopped it had her life depended on it.

Beside what she felt now her desire for Greg was a pale insignificance. Shaking, aroused to an unbearable pitch, she watched from beneath her lashes as Alex divested himself of his clothes. He moved with an animal grace that emphasised the strength of the muscles beneath the olive skin; when he turned to the bed there was an almost febrile glitter in the dark, hooded eyes.

The bed gave beneath his weight. Slowly she reached out and touched his face, found tiny beads of moisture on his upper lip and forehead. Then his head came down and she moaned as his mouth and hands, working in concert, forced her to realise just how sensual a being she was.

A long time—for ever—later she heard herself pleading, begging him for release from the unbearable hunger that he had roused. Her body was on fire for him, moving with reckless abandon beneath him, her hands clasped across his back as she tried to guide him.

'My God,' he muttered, breathing heavily, the fierce glitter in the narrowed eyes overwhelming her, 'you have a talent for this, darling. I can see how a man could lose his head!'

Christabel moaned, twisting, her lashes fluttering, her mouth dry. She was suffering—hurting—in agony! and then as she cried out the pain eased, replaced by a throbbing warmth which grew as she found the courage to move with him. Gasping, crushed by the driving ferocity of his body yet safe as she had never been before, sensations exploded within her and she heard him groan something as his body clenched and then relaxed, the weight of it pushing her deep into the bed.

A long time later she said in a small voice, 'You're heavy.'

'And you,' he said harshly, 'deserve a damned good hiding.'

He knew, of course. A moment after he had made himself master of her body she had felt the sudden spasm of rejection. If it had been possible he would have left her, but by then it was too late. The passion which had overwhelmed her had him in thrall also.

Now he rolled over on to his side and dragged her chin around with hard, hurting fingers. The dark eyes were angry.

'You stupid little *idiot*!' he muttered through lips that barely moved. 'Why?'

Why? How could she answer that? She didn't even know why herself. Reaction was making her shiver, but pride kept her still beneath the condemnation of his glare.

'Because I'm a stupid little idiot, I suppose. I'm sorry if I wasn't up to expectations, but no one could have had a more skilful lover for the first time.'

'There is,' he told her between clenched teeth, 'a mild sadism in initiating a virgin which is supposed to be pleasurable, even titillating. I've never experienced it before. Believe it or not, I don't make a practice of going to bed with virgins, even those who resemble nothing so much as conniving little flirts. Tell me, what do you have in mind now? An ongoing affair, or was this meant to be a one-night stand?'

'All that I have in mind,' she returned steadily, very pale beneath his contempt, 'is my own bed.'

'Then let's get you there.'

While Christabel climbed back into her pretty, crushed dress Alex left the enormous, shadowy bedroom, reappearing a few minutes later clad entirely in black. Neither spoke until they were back in the car.

Then he said, 'I don't suppose it occurred to you to take any precautions?'

'No.' By now the shame she had anticipated was setting in full. It was with an effort that she held her hands still in her lap.

He didn't seem surprised. 'I hope you have no little schemes up your sleeve.' And when she stared blankly at the cutting line of his profile he went on harshly, 'Such as living at my expense for the next sixteen years.'

'I don't——' When realisation struck her she went white, her voice cracking with outrage. 'How—how *dare* you! Why, you—you——'

'Swine?' he supplied grimly. 'It's been done before,

Christabel, but don't try it with me. I'm not easily trapped.'

'You can go to hell!' she snapped, humiliation scorching through her with such force that it resembled anger. Although the cold menace in his voice frightened her she forced herself to say, 'I haven't—I wouldn't——'

'I know you haven't, but whether you would or not remains to be seen.' As the car turned into the street where she lived he asked coolly, 'You aren't crying, are you?'

'No,' she spat, 'I am not. I do not intend to cry, not now, not later. I am not prone to crying.'

Surprisingly he laughed. 'A woman of spirit!' The car drew in to the kerb; he got out and locked it before saying, 'Here, give me your key.'

'It's all right,' she told him, but he took it from her hand and opened the street door, then escorted her up the stairs until they arrived outside the flat.

'This is it,' she said, and because there seemed nothing else to say added ridiculously, 'Thank you.'

He laughed, the cold antagonism giving way to wry amusement. 'And thank you, Christabel. *"The lovely lady Christabel"*. Later on in the same poem it says that she was *"Beautiful exceedingly"*. Appropriate. I'm sorry if I wasn't grateful enough for the gift you gave me.' He turned her and kissed her, gently on the mouth, softly on the forehead. 'I'll be seeing you. Goodnight.'

An hour later in the grey pre-dawn light she said to the taxi-driver, 'The airport, please. The international terminal,' and sat with hands folded on her lap, not looking back. And it was not of Greg that she thought as the vehicle moved through the silent streets.

CHAPTER THREE

'ICE-C'EAM!' Scott's voice lifted in demand. 'Kirsty, I *want* ice-c'eam!'

Christabel grinned down into his flushed little face. 'And just what would Mummy say if I fed you up on ice-cream so close to lunch?'

'Good boy,' he retorted before breaking into charming little boy's laughter. 'Good boy, Scottie.'

From behind the counter Mrs Upcott said comfortably, 'It's all right, Kirsty. Mrs Grieves usually buys him a little one. You always eat all your lunch, don't you, Scotty?'

'Yes,' he said promptly.

Christabel grinned, well aware of her little half-brother's insatiable appetite. During the months she had spent at home she had become almost a substitute mother for him. Elaine had been very ill both before and after the birth of their tiny sister.

He was so hot, the little hand in hers damp and sticky, tiny beads of moisture standing out on his short, freckled nose. Her mind was made up by the knowledge that ahead of them lay half an hour's drive along a dusty road. For a moment she thought wistfully of sealed thoroughfares and motorways, but banished the memory immediately. It was no use hankering for the amenities of the city when her stepmother needed her here. And life in this small New Zealand community where they still called her the Kirsty of her childhood was the breathing space she had needed so badly.

Next year she would go south to Auckland University and start her law course. Until then it was pleasant to revert back to her childhood life, resuming her father's name of Grieves instead of the Evans which

37

had been her mother's maiden name, cutting her hair
short so that the startling red waves had grown into
their natural colour and texture, a brown the colour of
a polished acorn which fitted like a close cap to the
small, proudly held head.

'What sort do you want, then?' she asked now, lifting
Scott up so that he could see the bins of ice cream.

'I want a pink one,' he said, then, 'No, look, Kirsty,
there's a *green* one!'

It looked virulent, but even as he noted it Scott's eyes
passed on to the next container and he hesitated, a
grubby finger wavering. From behind came the sound
of movement as someone else entered the little shop.

'This,' Christabel said to Mrs Upcott' is going to take
some time. We'll wait.'

The shopkeeper smiled sympathetically at Scott's
absorbed face and moved away.

'Yes?' she asked in her usual pleasant way.

'A *Herald*, please.' The deep voice was pleasant but cool.

Scott wriggled suddenly as the fingers which held him
clenched with painful force into his skin. 'Don't,
Mummy!' he protested, until Christabel lowered him to
the floor, bending over so that her bloodless face was
hidden.

For months that voice had haunted her dreams,
sensual and deep, then the quick whiplash of contempt,
the memory of which even now brought the blood
rushing back to her skin as the small transaction was
made, the newspaper handed over, the cash register
whirred, and the shrill bell tinkled as he left the shop.

Beside her Scott rambled on, his treble voice softly
fretful at her peculiar behaviour. Finally he said, 'The
green one, please, I want the green one, Mummy.'

It wasn't the first time he had called her that. He was
too small at four to understand that his adored Kirsty
was his half-sister and that there was only eight years'
difference between her and his mother, and his mind
tended to race ahead of his speech and on occasion he

got them mixed up. Elaine's illness had meant that the responsibility for him devolved on Christabel and quite often she answered to Mummy.

She was thankful for it now. If Alex Thomassin's shrewd eyes had noticed some resemblance between the half-witted creature who had seduced him a year ago and the leggy woman in faded shorts and an old shirt in this small shop in New Zealand's far North, surely Scott's innocent mistake would have put paid to any suspicion. Not only was there the difference in hair colour and style, but she was a few pounds heavier, no longer the too-slender girl who had stepped exhausted from the jumbo jet at Auckland and worried herself sick for three weeks until her body had reassured her that that night of incredible folly was going to leave her unscathed.

More or less unscathed, anyway, if she could discount the shame and the bitter regret that she had allowed Greg's betrayal to push her into such an outrageous reaction. Since the age of sixteen when she had realised her physical appeal, she had wanted to give her husband the responses of an untouched, untaught body. Her reckless stupidity had deprived her of that.

Mrs Upcott's voice intruded pleasantly on these rapid uncomfortable recollections.

'Made up your mind, sweetie?' she asked, then as she scooped a sphere of lurid ice-cream she remarked, 'I wonder who that was? I saw him look you over, Kirsty. He looked quite disappointed when young feller-me-lad here called you Mummy.'

Her chuckle invited complicity. It took an effort, but Christabel forced a smile and a banal response.

'He's not local, then?'

'Afraid not. Did you get a good look at him?' At Christabel's headshake she pursed her lips slightly. 'A pity. Tall dark and handsome was created for him! No, he was probably just passing through. Up for the big game fishing contest, I suppose.'

Christabel nodded. It seemed likely that Alex Thomassin would be over for the fishing competition a little farther up the coast.

'Ah well, good luck to him, then,' she said lightly. 'Ready to go, Scott?'

And with his mouth rapidly turning green and his hand tucked in hers she walked along the footpath, welcoming the shade cast by the shop verandah. Late summer it might be, but it was still hot enough for the heat to beat up from the road, causing tiny wavering mirages above the short strip of tarseal. Te Takapu was a small seaside settlement, too small for a hotel, just a narrow stretch of dust-free road between shops, a hall built to commemorate the dead in two world wars and a garage, with a jetty pushing out into the harbour.

It was the garage which caught Christabel's eyes. By the pumps stood a grey Range Rover and beside it, watching the attendant as she filled the petrol tank, was Alex Thomassin.

Sunlight struck tawny red scintillations from his head; his stance, hands in the pockets of casual trousers, revealed the breadth of his shoulders and the long, lean strength of his legs.

A sudden wave of colour shamed Christabel by its intensity. Fumbling, furious with herself at the vivid recollections which the sight of him had summoned from her subconscious, she opened the door of her father's big old Holden. As if attracted by the movement his head swung around and he watched as she put Scott into his safety seat.

Stiff-faced, her hands wet with perspiration, she pushed sunglasses on. Alex could not recognise her! Why should he? The last person he would be expecting to see in Te Takapu, across the stormy Tasman Sea from Australia, was Christabel Evans who had provided him with a few hours of sensual pleasure.

With head flung back she climbed behind the wheel. She had to wipe her hands dry on a tissue before she turned the key, but her confidence had returned enough for her to carelessly return a wave to Sally, the garage attendant.

A quick glance in the mirror revealed that he was talking to her, the dark red head bent. Christabel noted the flash of his smile and forced her eyes back to the road ahead. No doubt he was just flirting lightly with Sally, who was pert and pretty and single, but even if for some strange reason he enquired about one Christabel Evans he would meet with total blankness. Here there was no such person. Kirsty Grieves, who lives on a remote farm with her father and stepmother, was a world removed from the elegant, brittle fashion model who had thought herself so madly in love with Greg that she had allowed a dreadful bitterness to overset the principles of a lifetime.

I *will not* let this—this beastly coincidence bother me, she vowed through gritted teeth as she concentrated on the road. She had suffered enough for a night's folly, weeping tears of shame, wondering hopelessly why she, so in love with Greg, could find ecstasy in another man's body.

It had taken her months to face the fact that what she felt for Greg had been nothing more than the same physical attraction which Alex Thomassin had used to sweep her off her feet—with her enthusiastic cooperation!

And that discovery had brought self-contempt of the worst sort, undermining her self-esteem so that it was still difficult for her to accept her own worth. Elaine had worried because her lovely stepdaughter appeared to have no interest in men until, more to please her than anything else, Christabel had accepted invitations from Nate Kennedy, the local vet. Now they had a friendly, placid relationship which was as much as she felt capable of managing. No more ecstasies for her, she thought grimly.

The long road stretched, blinding white between

hakea hedges and eucalyptus and pine plantations. Behind them was the government block, which had once been an enormous swamp. Now, drained and fenced and grassed, it was well on the way to becoming fifteen productive farms.

Beyond that was another area of wilderness and then Rangitatau, the gate to heaven.

Christabel took her foot from the accelerator and engaged a lower gear. Around and behind the car a great cloud of dust hung on the still air. From now on the road deteriorated into something only a little better than a track, but she knew it so well that it held no fears for her, not even the railless bridges which seemed only six inches wider than the wheels. On either side the stunted manuka scrub was white with dust, the little stream revealing by its dark mysterious colour its source in the peat swamps.

To the south rose hills, old, consolidated sand dunes five hundred feet high which sheltered Rangitatau from the south and west. Those which belonged to the station were easily distinguished because they had been planted in pines, giving an oddly Brothers Grimm aspect to a landscape which otherwise could only belong to New Zealand. The dark green of the pines contrasted with the drab olive of the scrub, dusted now with manuka flowers like snow on dark foliage.

Christabel flicked a glance into the rear-vision mirror, saw through her dust a plume which denoted another vehicle and frowned. There was nothing else out here but Rangitatau.

'Car?' Scott said cheerfully, twisting around to see.

'Yes, darling, a car.'

A prickle of unease made itself felt, was instantly banished. It was stupid to allow that unnerving encounter this morning to make her nervous. Almost certainly the car behind was some friend of Elaine's, or a tourist who just wanted to see what and where Rangitatau was.

Sure enough, a few miles farther on the second cloud of dust had vanished. Tourists, she thought cheerfully, who had decided that the bad road was too much. Singing 'This Old Man' she and Scott passed by the remaining miles to Rangitatau.

At the top of the low hill which separated Rangitatau from the rest of the world she stopped the car and with Scott walked a little way across the short, springy sward, her eyes roaming this loved scene.

The Maori who had christened the place knew what he was about, she thought appreciatively. Rangitatau, the gate to heaven, was an inlet with two rocky headlands forming barriers against the often turbulent Pacific Ocean. Inside the Gates four exquisite beaches formed an almost completely circular harbour, each beach separated by low, steep headlands, green-grassed or bush-covered. In ancient days each hill had been a fortified *pa*, home and safety to the Maori tribe who had lived here.

Two of the beaches backed onto land still owned by the descendants of that tribe. The other two, and a couple of thousand acres of good beef country, was Donald Grieves' patrimony, farmed for three generations by the family, perhaps one day to be Scott's.

Here Donald had brought his English first wife, here she had borne their only child and spent the years in loneliness and discontent until finally she had fled to Australia where there were theatres and fashion and the busy, bustling life she had missed so badly.

She had never known how hungry Christabel had been for Rangitatau, its wild beauty forever printed on her heart like an image of Paradise. Mother and daughter had loved one another, but their needs were far apart and Brenda Evans had never realised just how distant they were.

Well, Christabel was satisfied now. Her time here had brought the healing she had needed so badly.

'There's that car,' Scott observed cheerfully, turning to point.

Sure enough the drone of an engine intruded on the peace. Christabel's head jerked; she was not in the least surprised to see the Range Rover pull into sight.

Her first instinct, born of panic, to run for the Holden, had to be squashed. He would think she was mad and he was too shrewd for her to wish to rouse any suspicion. Pray God he was only sightseeing.

But there was an air of purpose to the tall figure which climbed out of the stationary vehicle and came across the grass to where they waited, Scott alert but not alarmed, Christabel so tense that she could feel the sharp pull of protesting muscles.

'Good morning,' he said, giving her long bare legs a swift, admiring survey. 'Miss—Grieves, isn't it?'

A muscle moved in the golden silk of her throat. 'Yes, Kirsty Grieves. How——?'

Those dark grey eyes smiled down at her, appreciative, mocking. 'I asked the very obliging young lady at the garage,' he told her, and amused comprehension danced in his glance. He knew she had seen him with Sally.

Stiffly, still afraid yet reassured by the total lack of recognition in the strong features, she returned, 'And you are . . .?'

'Alex Thomassin.' He held out his hand.

Slowly, reluctantly, she put hers into it, remembering once before doing exactly the same thing. But this time he didn't kiss it, nor did his face reveal any of the sexual awareness of that first meeting. After a quick handshake she pulled her hand away.

A thread of tension spun between them, broken by Scott who held out his small, green-stained paw and said plaintively, 'Shake mine, too. I'm Scott.'

She had to give him full marks for his attitude. With no sign of patronage his hand enveloped Scott's and he smiled. Dazzled by this splendid stranger, Scott smiled back; Christabel saw the worshipping expression on her little brother's face with a sinking heart. What on earth did this man possess, so potent that it worked equally well with women and small children? It was not just that charisma that sent her nerves prickling, the physical attributes of height and looks and a lazy confidence barely hiding the thrusting arrogance beneath.

She gave up, wariness lowering her lashes as he turned back to her. Good manners indicated that she take off her sunglasses; her instinct of self-preservation bade her leave them firmly on. Instinct won out.

'Can I help you?' she asked politely. 'As you can see, the road ends at our gate at the foot of the hill. Do you want to see Dad?'

He lifted a straight dark brow. 'I'm just touring; but I'm curious about the difference between one farm and the other.' His beautifully shaped hand gestured from the smooth green acres of the station to the rugged, much paler pastures through the boundary.

'Well, Dad could tell you much better than I,' she said, caution keeping her tones cool. 'But the land next to ours is Maori land and for years the law has made it incredibly difficult for them to do anything with it. Very recently they've been able to make headway. Soon it should look as good as ours.'

He nodded, surveying the panorama before them before turning to face the sea. 'It looks as though no foul weather ever comes here.'

'Well, it often gets quite rough in winter,' she said politely.

Scott pointed. 'I've got a boat,' he confided. 'Down there.'

Alex Thomassin nodded. 'Can you swim, young man?'

'Yes.'

'He was swimming before he could walk,' Christabel told him drily.

'And you? Did you swim before you could walk?'

The question was made idly and accompanied by another smile as though he could think of nothing better to do than flirt with the nearest unattached woman, but it made Christabel cautious.

'Yes,' she said shortly, and took Scott's hand in hers, prepared to take herself off as speedily as she could.

'It seems incredible that there's been no development,' he mused, apparently losing interest in his companions as the dark gaze swung across Rangitatau.

Christabel shrugged. 'How could there be? Apart from the road, which you must agree is a shocker, there are only the two properties down here. Dad certainly wouldn't permit development of ours and the *hapu*—the tribe—who own the other land have been in no position to allow it.' She added crisply, 'Besides, like us, this is their homeland, their resting place. It's so wild and beautiful—just imagine it with hotels and motels everywhere, the peace and serenity destroyed—another Surfers!'

'Have you been to Surfers?' The question flicked like a whiplash through the warm air.

Almost Christabel trembled. Beneath the dark lenses of her sunglasses her eyes flew to meet the cool relentlessness of his. A lie trembled on her lips, but instinct warned her in time.

'Yes,' she said coldly.

'Did you enjoy it?'

For a moment her teeth clamped on her lower lip. With an immense reluctance she conceded, 'Yes, I love it.' She looked up, met the laughter in his eyes and smiled wryly. 'But not here, Mr Thomassin. Rangitatau is not the Gold Coast.'

'No, that was mainly swamp before it was developed,' he agreed.

At the same moment Scott called gleefully. 'There's Daddy!'

Both protagonists swung to see Donald Grieves come over the top of the hill on his horse, two eager, bright-eyed dogs racing ahead to greet Scott with the ease and familiarity of long friendship.

Of course Christabel had to introduce the two men, and of course Donald asked Alex down to the homestead.

'I saw you from the hill over there,' he said, his blue eyes clear and far-sighted as a sailor's. 'Wondered what you were doing.'

'Admiring the view,' Alex told him smoothly.

And that was that. Elaine greeted him with pleasure, her pale skin pinking at the compliment he paid her. Only Christabel noticed that quick, unsparing glance which had taken in the older woman's fragility.

Oddly enough she was no longer afraid of being recognised. She might have never forgotten the timbre of his voice; it was only too obvious that he had no recollection of her at all.

Probably, she thought scornfully, because there had been so many women since then. Gossip made much of his prowess as a lover; swift fugitive colour touched her throat and cheeks as she put herself on a par with the other women in his life. Why should he remember a one-night stand, even if she had been the only virgin he'd taken?

'You go and talk to him,' she said to Elaine in the kitchen. 'I'll get lunch.'

Elaine looked torn. 'Well, it's all ready. Quiche and salad and stewed peaches to follow. How lucky that you made bread this morning, Kirsty! Oh, and there's custard for the peaches.' She hesitated. 'It's a very *country* lunch.'

Meaning that even in the casual denims he wore Alex Thomassin was clearly a person for whom one made an effort. Well, with the money he had and that sophistication of course he was.

Christabel gave her a quick hug. 'Country or not, you're a good cook and he'll love it. Now, go and flirt with him.'

Quick laughter caught in Elaine's throat. 'Recognise his sort, do you? I'm sure that he'd rather flirt with you.'

'Do me a favour, will you?' Christabel knew that she sounded offhand, but for the life of her she couldn't manage anything else. 'Don't mention that I've modelled.'

Her stepmother nodded, her glance shrewd. 'You do recognise his sort, don't you?'

'I'm afraid so.' Imperceptibly she straightened her shoulders, looked amused and wry at the same time. 'Well, let's face it, why shouldn't he be a flirt? I'll bet no woman ever said no to him in his life, and I'm including his mother in that. He's bound to be spoiled. And quite frankly, I don't want to have to fend him off.'

'In that case,' said Elaine with a swift chuckle, 'I'd change those shorts for something a little more circumspect. I saw his very appreciative glance at your legs. What's he doing here?'

'I don't know.'

'Idle curiosity?' But Elaine answered her own question. 'No, whatever he is he's not the type to do anything idly. A more forceful character it would be hard to imagine!'

'I saw him in town.'

Quite why she volunteered the information Christabel didn't know.

The older woman laughed. 'Perhaps he followed you out.'

'Hardly.' But when Elaine had left the room Christabel found herself frowning. Surely he wouldn't have—no, the idea was ridiculous. Alex Thomassin had no need to follow women—they chased him, drawn by his magnetic personality and those superb good looks. Oh, and the money too, she thought cynically.

As she tore greenstuffs up for the salad and mixed the dressing she tried to blank her mind to the queries that hunted themselves around her brain. It didn't work, of course. Through the screened windows she could hear them talking out on the terrace, just far enough away so that the words were only sounds.

He had not recognised her, she would swear to it. No man, not even one as good as Alex at controlling his features, could have looked at her like that if he had recognised her. She had been prepared for a give-away blankness, or shock or a knowing smile, any one of which would have spelt recognition.

But the lazy glance had been appreciative, pleasantly mocking, the exact glance of a man who liked women and had just seen one who interested him. Only that way would he have looked had he never seen her before, sparked with a certain pleasant awareness that he was male and she was female, that her legs were long and brown and well shaped, her waist trim and her breasts pleasantly rounded, her face attractive enough to warrant a second glance.

No, he could not have any idea that she was anything other than what she seemed, the daughter of the house. Now, if only Elaine could steer Donald away from any mention of those years spent modelling—but then, although he was proud of his daughter and loved her Donald would have preferred her to use her intelligence some other way; they had discussed her ambition to be a lawyer and he had offered to help her achieve it. No, Donald wasn't exactly proud of the fact that she had modelled for a living and would hardly be likely to refer to it.

Suddenly shaky, she ran a hand over her clammy forehead. It was hot. A glance through the glass oven door revealed that the quiche was almost ready; she set the big kauri table in the morning room, then went down to her own room to change into a dress, a plain and subdued cotton in a shade of mint green. A quick touch of lip-gloss and a comb passed through the smooth cap of her hair was all that she ventured in the way of prettying up. She was not going to do anything which might be construed as trying to attract his attention, she decided grimly.

The cold feeling in her stomach stayed. It was fear, of course, and with it there was a kind of sick humiliation. The thing which had hurt the most about the affair of Alex Thomassin was the frightening loss of self-respect. The girl who had behaved like some half-witted courtesan in his arms had terrified Christabel, for if she was capable once of such amoral wilfulness it could happen again.

For months she had watched her every reaction with an icy caution, afraid that she would feel again that suffocating tide of desire in response to some man's approach.

Thank God, it hadn't happened. And she had just begun to accept that it might have been an aberration brought on by misery and exhaustion and champagne when he had to come back into her life, a hideous complication in an existence which she had only now begun to hope might remain calm and ordered. And without being aware of it she had made the mental proviso that for that so desired calmness and order there must be no more succumbing to passion or love.

'Let's eat outside,' said Elaine, suddenly appearing. She was pink and glowing, her expression slightly bemused. 'It's so hot, I think we must be in for rain.'

The table on the terrace was large and, unfortunately, round in shape, which meant that there was no way to escape Alex's glance. Not that he stared, or made his interest blatantly obvious. He had superb manners, as well as that devastating charm; it was utterly infuriating for Christabel to watch as together and individually he dazzled them all, from Scott to her father.

Appetite gone, she forced herself to eat. Not for anything would she show her tension or her animosity. But not even willpower could summon up her normal cheerful attitude and she knew that Elaine and Donald were puzzled by her unusual quietness.

When they had finished she cleared the table and made tea; even there he fitted in. When she asked if he'd prefer coffee he smiled that lazy, well-behaved smile and said blandly, 'No, not at all. Australians are great tea-drinkers, too, you know.'

Over tea Donald asked, 'You're here on holiday, I gather.'

'Yes.' He shrugged slightly, drawing Christabel's unwilling attention to the breadth of the shoulders beneath the cotton.

Fragments of memories obtruded, of those shoulders above her, and were firmly suppressed.

'Any particular place, or just looking around?' This was Elaine, her friendly interest robbing the question of impertinence.

'Just prowling around. This is an undiscovered part of the country, isn't it? I don't think I've ever seen a more beautiful coastline, and yet I've never heard it mentioned before and you're obviously not geared for tourists.'

'Rarely see them.' Donald sat back in his chair, his gaze going to the exquisite view before them.

Between the sheltering pohutukawa trees the waters of the bay glittered like blue and silver lamé. Only two beaches were visible from where they sat, each crescent was warmly pink in the sunlight, darker where the tide had reached that morning. Down on the beach a small flock of oyster-catchers moved like overcoated men, sombre in the sunlight. The Gates were silhouetted against the lambent blue of the sky, high, their rugged flanks pitted with the remains of trenches. At the far end of the homestead bay another, smaller *pa* stood, the grass over it revealing clearly the telltale lines of more trenches which had once held rows of enormous sharpened stakes as a further defence. The *pa* on the north headland had the reputation of never having been taken by an enemy.

Christabel could remember a picnic up there one day

with the Panapa children. Old Mr Panapa had come
with them and had told them stories of their forebears,
brave, barbaric and splendid in their pride. The
beautiful Maori words had rolled smoothly from his
tongue and she had envied her friends their ancestry,
saying childishly: 'I wish my grandfather had been like
that instead of just an ordinary old farmer.' And the
Panapa children had looked proud and smug, but Mr
Panapa had sighed and said gently in English, 'Well,
those days were for everyone, once. Long, long ago for
your people, Kirsty, not so long ago for us.'

For a long time he had sat, staring out to sea with
eyes which saw much, while the children had fought a
splendid battle in the filled-in ditches of the old
trenches.

Shortly after that the Panapa family had been forced
to leave their home so that young Mr Panapa could
find work, but they often came back for holidays,
although their house in the next bay was little better
than a ruin now.

Sighing for days long gone when life had been
simpler, Christabel dragged her attention back to the
conversation.

To find Donald pointing out the virtues of their
special patch of country. 'Fishing,' he said. 'Well, it's
not fished out yet like other places. You can still get
into the boat and come back with enough for you and
your neighbours. And mako and swordfish come
through this way if you're keen on big-game fishing.
Then for a holiday this can't be beaten. Some quirk of
climate gives us more hours of sunlight and lower
rainfall than farther north or south. And these are not
the only beaches—there are plenty of really beautiful
ones farther north.'

'Not necessarily a good thing for you, such a
climate,' Alex commented quietly.

Donald nodded. 'We've another station inland in the
hills. It's a help.'

'With all these advantages, why no tourists?'

Spreading his hands, Donald said cheerfully, 'Well, the coastline is all privately owned or Maori land and we're a long way from anywhere. Our roads put off all but the most determined.'

Alex made a grimace. 'Yes, as I discovered,' he said drily, the dark opacity of his glance flicking to Christabel's face.

Hastily she composed her expression, hoping it wasn't revealing any of the unease she felt. It was stupid to let her natural wariness make her feel there was an ulterior motive for Alex's interest.

'Well,' Donald said slowly, 'if you haven't any fixed plans why not stay here for a few days and see what we have to offer?'

That quick glance flicked back to Christabel's face. Did he see her dismay, or realise that the involuntary jerk of her fingers which set the tea-cup she held clattering down on to the table was caused by her father's invitation?

'That's very kind of you.'

The deep cool voice hesitated and Elaine said swiftly, 'Do stay, Mr Thomassin, if you think you'd enjoy our quiet life.' Smiling, she added, 'Australians aren't the only ones famous for their hospitality, you know.'

His smile flashed out, warm, subversive. 'I'd enjoy that very much,' he said without so much as a glance at Christabel. 'Thank you.'

Stunned, almost as bewildered as she would have been if Donald had beaten her, Christabel got to her feet.

'Scott's nearly asleep,' she said, her voice unnaturally level. 'I'll just put him to bed.'

And with the warm little body restless against her she carried him off to his bedroom.

'Man going to stay?' he enquired sleepily.

'Yes darling, for a little while.'

He gave her his enchanting grin and a moist warm

kiss. 'Good,' he said with a sigh of drowsy satisfaction, 'I can show him mine boat.'

Which was all very well, but of no consolation to Christabel. She felt as though Elaine and Donald had betrayed her, and the feeling was no less strong for being totally illogical. What on earth had possessed her father to invite a total stranger into his home on such short acquaintance? Elaine might talk about hospitality, but although nobody could accuse Donald of being churlish he usually waited until he knew people before making them free of Rangitatau.

It was that infernal charm, she thought unfairly, that aura Alex projected so effortlessly. Just from looking at him nobody would believe that he was as tough as rawhide under that sophisticated smiling surface. Well, not until you noticed that the cut of the jaw was hard and uncompromising, and the eyes met yours with the kind of challenge which was a threat in itself.

'Oh, *bother*!' she exclaimed inadequately, struck by another thought.

Elaine would put him in the guest-room, which was right next door to her stepdaughter's, and she knew that she couldn't bear the thought of him being just through four inches of wall, or whatever thickness they made walls when the homestead was built. She wouldn't be able to sleep at night for listening.

Which left only one thing to do.

CHAPTER FOUR

'WHY Great-grandmother's room?' Elaine asked curiously as they did the dishes.

Donald and Alex were out on the station. It hadn't helped Christabel's equilibrium to discover that he was a superb rider, obviously taught by stockmen, for he rode with the relaxed style which looked so casual and made long days in the saddle ease past with as little stress and fatigue as possible.

Christabel wrung the dishcloth dry as though it were somebody's neck. 'Because it's bigger. He looks as though he needs room to move round in.'

It was hardly an adequate answer but Elaine, the darling, left it there. 'You don't really mind your father asking him, do you?'

The dishcloth was draped over the window bar where sun and fresh air would sweeten it. 'No, of course not.'

'Well, I'm glad, because you must admit, Kirsty, he's a fascinating man.'

Oh, yes, she knew, only two well she knew, just how fascinating he was. Using the word in its proper meaning, of course. According to the Concise Oxford Dictionary *'To deprive a victim of the power of escape or resistance by one's look or presence.'* Yes, fascinating was exactly the word to describe Alex Thomassin.

Aloud she said in a tight wooden voice, 'Well, he'll be a change, anyway. A being from another world, almost.'

'Did you mind leaving it?' Elaine asked tentatively. 'You've never said. I was so grateful to see you that I'm afraid I've been selfish. Once or twice it's occurred to me that you might miss the glamour and the stimulation, but you fitted in here so smoothly, as though you were happy to be back.'

'I was. I am,' Christabel told her promptly. 'I love Rangitatau. Every night for years I wept in longing for it. My life in Australia was exciting, but it didn't hurt me in the least to leave.' Hesitating, she added with an odd shyness, 'In fact, you could say I used you and Rangitatau as a refuge. I needed to come here.'

Her stepmother nodded, her kind eyes sympathetic as they rested on Christabel's averted profile. 'I'd guessed as much. A man, I suppose, it usually is. That's why I came up this way myself. Then I met your father and suddenly nothing but he mattered. Perhaps the same will happen with you. Nate Kennedy seems very interested. Don says he hasn't had such tender loving care for the stock *ever* before!'

Christabel smiled but shook her head. 'Nate is nice and I'm very fond of him, but there's nothing in the least romantic in our relationship.'

'Pity,' her stepmother said slyly as she put an assortment of bread and butter plates into a cupboard. 'He's on holiday at the moment, isn't he? Where is he?'

'Climbing in the Southern Alps. He'll be back in a week.'

Elaine nodded. She liked Nate and she was by no means as convinced as Kirsty about the state of their relationship. Nate's glances were giveaways, she thought, very soft and tender whenever he looked at Kirsty. Whoever the man was who had put that bruised, desolate look in Kirsty's eyes should have been shot, but perhaps it was necessary for her to burn her wings in the fires of passion before she learnt the worth of the kind of enduring secure love Elaine had found with Donald Grieves. At the moment Kirsty was wary and her reaction to Alex Thomassin was revealing. Whoever had hurt her so must have been of the same type, experienced, aware of his effect on people, basically hard and clever and dynamic but covering the granite core with a cloak of lazy sophistication.

Give her time and she would recover from the

disillusionment, and Nate would get his chance. Elaine
liked the tall, handsome vet, with the warm smile and
the gentle hands, and she thought that whatever Kirsty
might think, he more than liked her. Yes, given time,
perhaps Kirsty would learn to love him.

Aware of the trend of her stepmother's thoughts
Christabel grinned. 'Stop matchmaking,' she teased.
'You've got that devious, absorbed look that terrifies
the life out of any man who sees it! I'm perfectly happy
the way things are.'

Elain's chuckle was deep and infectious. 'Well, my
dear, I'll promise not to embarrass you when Nate's
around. Shall we take the children down to the beach
when they wake up? It's such a beautiful day and I'd
like to get a little more tan before winter arrives.'

'What are we going to have for dinner?'

'I thought we'd prepare that before we went down.
Roast lamb done the Kashmiri way, with green ginger
and cumin and garam masala. I'll roast potatoes with it
and we can have a green salad. And if you, darling
sweet stepdaughter, will make a cold lemon soufflé,
which you do so well, I'll whip up a zucchini soup in the
blender. It will be nicely chilled if I put it in the deep-
freeze. Only for heaven's sake don't let me forget it, like
I did with that wine cask!'

It was fun to share a reminiscent chuckle, fun to
work together in the big farmhouse kitchen which
Donald had had modernised for his first, English wife.

And when dinner was prepared they took the
children, Scott proudly bearing bucket and spade, and
set off down the wide farm track to the beach. From the
lawn in front of the house there was another, shorter
way down, but it was narrow and steep and
manoeuvring baby Stephanie in her carry-cot down it
required dexterity and strength which neither of the
women possessed.

The beach basked tranquilly in the afternoon sun,
pinky-beige in colour, small waves making tentative

forays across the sand. While Elaine spread out the rugs beneath the kindly shade of a pohutukawa Christabel set the carry-cot down, playing peep-bo with the baby until she gave one of her enchanting chuckles, tiny starfish hands waving before the delighted pink face.

'I love you, you delectable little scrap,' Christabel said, and picked her out of the carry-cot, cuddling her against her breast. 'Darling little wicked one, deep dyed in villainy . . .' The extravagant nonsense rolled on, both participants enjoying it hugely until Scott called for help with the decoration of his sand castle and Elaine accepted her daughter for more loving.

'*Not* that kind of shell,' Scott told her seriously as she picked up a ramshorn. 'Like this, darling Kirsty,' showing her a tiny silvery paua.

'But, darling Scott, there aren't very many of that sort and there are scads of ramshorns,' she protested, knowing full well that she wasn't going to be let off with such a poor excuse. Scott had very definite ideas on the decoration of his castles.

'We'll find them,' he told her confidently, scrambling to his feet. 'Come on!'

Smiling, she took the wet, sandy little hand and set off with him towards the rocks where they were more likely to find the spoils of the last storm.

The high voice chattered on as they sifted through the multitudes of shells, asking, commenting, occasionally gloating when he knew the name of one and Christabel had forgotten, slowly adding to the little pile of oval shells, their rough outer surface hiding an exquisite iridescence of green and pink and silver, more colourful than mother-of-pearl, as pretty as opals.

'What you call it?' he demanded, holding another deceptively fragile shell up in triumph.

'Silvery paua,' she told him. 'It's real name is *hihiwa*. Can you say that?'

'*Hi-hi-wa.*' He pronounced the syllables carefully, his damp forehead wrinkled in concentration.

'Clever boy!' Mr Panapa had told her all the lovely euphonious Maori names for the shellfish and his thin, energetic wife had shown her how to gather and cook them.

Not for the first time Christabel wondered just how they liked their life in Auckland, they and all the other members of their tribe who were separated from the land they loved because it no longer gave them all that they needed. Remembering her own desolation at such a separation, she knew that they would hate it and long for their homeland with an aching hunger that greyed their days and made the nights lonely.

Life here satisfied something elemental in her, the peace and beauty fulfilling a need which the long years away had only repressed.

'Here's Daddy,' Scott said suddenly, staring along the beach. 'And the man.'

Sure enough the two horses were ambling back at the edge of the tide, tails flicking, ears twitching. Christabel stood up, hollow inside at the realisation that until Alex Thomassin went away—and surely he'd know not to stay more than a couple of days?—she would be continually assailed by this mixture of self-reproach and humiliation.

Why should she be so sensitive? It was like carrying an albatross around her neck, this intense reaction to his presence fuelled by what she could only see as a taint in her blood. Other women had affairs and never thought a thing about them; apparently men took what they could get whenever they could get it and there was no thought of self-contempt in the way they viewed the episodes. So why should she feel smirched and degraded by one night's stupidity?

And it wasn't just that. She had been telling the truth when she told Sarah that her mother's rather rigid attitude towards moral standards had been passed on to her. Deep inside her brain, or whatever part of her body her personality inhabited, she felt that she had betrayed

and comprised some essential part of her, making
herself a lesser person. It was not only the mechanical
process of losing her virginity, it was the fact that she
had been only too willing, in fact eager for it to happen.
Somehow, in spite of her supposed love for another
man, her body and mind had responded to a hot
sensuality which for a time overrode everything else, her
principles, her common sense, even her sanity.

Not again. Not *ever* again. Now that she was
forewarned she knew how to protect herself from that
shameful weakness. The aloofness she had shown must
be modified a little so as not to arouse Alex's hunting
instincts, but she must make it quite plain that she had
no interest in him as a man.

Allowing herself a regretful thought at Nate's
absence, she walked slowly back to where Elaine was
still cooing love words to her daughter. In a thin gold
bikini it was hard to appear dignified, but she tried for
it.

'Here come the men,' she said.

Elaine looked past her. 'Oh—oh *no!*'

Scott had not followed Christabel. Instead, forgetting
a whole set of stern instructions, he had run towards the
men on horseback, calling out to his father and waving.

'And Don's on that *stupid* toey Mac,' Elaine
moaned, scrambling to her feet, her face pale with
apprehension.

Sure enough the black stallion reared, backing into
Alex's gelding. Only then did Scott remember his
father's strict instructions and came to a frightened halt,
his little figure tragically fragile against the bulk of the
horses. For a moment the tableau seemed frozen on to
the glittering waters of the bay, Donald fighting his
horse's head away, Scott shrinking and still too close
for comfort.

And then the gelding swung into action. Swiftly and
with consummate horsemanship Alex swooped, grabbed
Scott and hauled him against himself as he set the

gelding up the beach away from the snorting, angry stallion and its sweating rider.

'Oh, thank God!' Elaine sighed, sinking back on to the rug.

Alex brought the gelding towards them, one strong arm around Scott, talking soothingly so that the scared white look gradually faded from the small face. It took all her strength for Christabel to walk down to them and receive Scott into her arms; she held him tightly for a moment, then set him down to run to his mother and stared up into Alex's face.

'Thank you,' she said, realising for the first time how totally inadequate a simple statement of heartfelt gratitude could be.

'He wasn't really in any danger,' he said, pitching his voice so that Elaine could hear it. 'It almost certainly looked a lot worse than it was. He had the sense to stop as soon as that mount of your father's started its tricks.' His voice dropped, became infused with a note of mocking intimacy. 'When you're afraid your eyes go a deep dark blue. Did you know?'

'I—yes, I've been told so before.' He was confusing her, half-closed eyes showing a thin gleam of colour behind the dense lashes which should have belonged to a woman.

He smiled with irony and swung from the saddle, saying coolly, 'Your stepmother looks as though she needs a hand.'

It was a relief to turn away to where Elaine had picked up the carry-cot. Although not heavy it was unwieldy and she staggered slightly as she came towards them, Scott firmly attached to one hand.

'Here. I'll take that,' Christabel scolded beneath her breath.

'No, I'll take it.' And Elaine meekly handed it and its precious contents over to the imperative hand Alex stretched out.

'Mrs Grieves, why don't you take Scott up on the

horse? I'll bring the baby up and Kirsty can stagger up under the rest of the paraphernalia.'

Alex's voice was light, but Elaine obeyed, after saying fervently, 'Thank you so much for picking this scamp up! Scott?'

'Thank you.' Scott's voice was extremely subdued, but he met his rescuer's eyes manfully. 'I was a silly twit, mine mummy said.'

'You were indeed.' Alex's free hand touched the tousled fair head. 'Never mind, you won't do it again, will you?'

'No, *never*,' Scott returned, so fervently that they all laughed, easing the tension.

Down at the tide line Donald had at last succeeded in bringing the black under control and came towards them, his face anxious beneath the hat that protected his skin from the northern sun. 'O.K.?' he shouted.

As Kirsty gave Elaine a leg-up on to the gelding she yelled, 'Fine!' then passed Scott up to sit comfortably in front of his mother.

'Then I'll take this idiot up first.' The black horse took off up the track as if all the dogs in Christendom were at its heels. Elaine frowned as she clucked to the gelding, following much more sedately. And, left alone with an Alex who stood gently swinging the carry-cot and watching her, Christabel folded the rug and gathered the flask of orange juice into the flax *kete*.

She felt clumsy and nervous, forcing herself to remember that to him she was just the daughter of the house, no one he knew or had ever met before.

A gull soared overhead, calling its strange forlorn cry. In the carry-cot Stephanie produced a series of interested cooing noises. Even at that age, apparently, Alex Thomassin had an effect on a woman, Christabel decided sourly as she came towards him, acutely conscious of the brevity of her attire. Had she known there was any possibility of meeting him she would have brought more than an old cotton tee-shirt to cover her bikini.

Too late now, but she would remember in future. He had been smiling down at the baby, but as Christabel trod heavily through the thick sand towards him he glanced up and watched her, his dark eyes for a moment coldly speculative as they swept the smooth contours of her body.

Then he smiled with a warm indolent charm and she remembered that she was going to be aloof but not too much so, so she smiled back, although it made her face ache to do it.

'How old are you, Kirsty?'

She shrugged. 'Twenty-two, Mr Thomassin.'

As they fell into step together to climb the track he said, 'I'm thirty-one, which makes me rather young to be slotted so firmly into your parents' generation. Would it hurt if you called me Alex?'

For some reason he was subjecting her to the full force of his magnetic appeal. Perhaps he just couldn't resist women!

The scornful little thought brought a green flash to her eyes, hastily hidden by the sweep of her lashes. 'No, of course not,' she replied politely.

Stephanie produced a gurgle and stared up so intently that her eyes crossed slightly.

'And what do you do? For a living?'

She shrugged, 'I help Elaine,' she said baldly. 'She's been sick. What do you do, Mr—Alex?'

Just momentarily his eyes narrowed, but his voice was bland as he answered. 'I'm a businessman.'

'A captain of industry?'

He grinned down at her. 'You don't sound as though you have a very high opinion of businessmen! Were you bitten by one once?' And as her reluctant smile could no longer be hidden he swung the carry-cot on to his other side so that it no longer separated them.

It seemed a move towards some sort of intimacy. Christabel moved sideways so that there was at least a foot between them. That Alex was aware of the little distancing gesture and its meaning she was certain, but she didn't care. She wanted nothing more to do with him. He had caused her enough bitter remorse to last a lifetime.

Long ago the first Grieves family had made a track up to the house on its little plateau from their lifeline, the beach, the only transport route they had in the days when the North was a wild and roadless place. The age-old pohutukawas hadn't been disturbed, but where their thick shade lessened there had been planted other trees, natives and exotics which were hardy enough to cope with salt spray and wind. Now they were tall, and between them the bright lilac-blue lily of the Nile flowered with its delectable name which Christabel was now teaching Scott. Agapanthus—a splendid name for a splendid plant with its great sunbursts of flowers held high on long thick stalks.

Edging the lawn beneath the silk trees and the jacarandas were hibiscuses, their immense crêpe flowers still glowing, vivid, almost garish. A gardenia bloomed against the wall of the house, the thick, heavily scented flowers creamy white against the glossy foliage.

Thanks to Elaine's green fingers a fragipani blossomed here in a sunny sheltered nook of the inner terrace; the framework of the garden was old, but Elaine's love of colour kept it gay even in the depths of winter. It was watered from a bore which had never run dry, not even in the worst of summers.

Alex Thomassin stopped as they came out through the small, hidden gate onto the sunny lawn. For a moment he stared around, looking his fill at the mellow old house. Unnoticed, Christabel eyed him, her gaze lingering on the strong framework of his face. He was beautiful, she thought carefully monitoring her reactions. Beautiful in a wholly masculine way, with the strength of perfect health and all of the assets a most unfair Fate could bestow on him, beginning with that magnificent bone structure, the wide shoulders and narrow hips, long legs and lean, strong hands.

A shiver prickled her skin. No, she must not remember just how gentle those hands could be, gentle and then suddenly fierce so that the pain was an extension of the gentleness and both were erotically exciting.

'Stephanie's hungry,' she said, a note of tension roughening her voice.

His gaze swung around to capture hers. For a moment it burned into her as though he knew what she was thinking and wanted her, too. Only for a moment, however.

'Then we'd better take her inside,' he said coolly.

It was an odd evening. Elaine made a little production of the dinner and they ate in the dining room with the best silver and the old, beautiful china which had been one of Great-grandmother Grieves' wedding presents. It was a superb meal, enhanced by good wine and the smell of the roses which someone had brought for Elaine several days ago. 'Autumn Delight', they were called, beautiful almost single flowers, creamy white with quaint yellow buds and vigorous red stamens like exclamation marks. Their scent was a vapour in the panelled room and they glowed against the warm wood of the kauri table.

Conversation flowed easily, as though they had all known each other for years. Elaine sparkled, her warmth and kindness so obvious that Christabel thought it was no wonder Alex's eyes rested so frequently on her. And Donald, stimulated by his guest's intelligence, exercised his dry wit. Dreamily, still cautious, Christabel said little, refusing more than a glass or two of wine and spending much of the evening staring into the crystal depths of her goblet.

It was Alex who was the pivot of the evening, his charm and intelligence and interest that stimulated them all. He was enchanting them as he had her, weaving a spell about them so that they seemed members of a magic circle.

What an asset for a businessman! Christabel thought drily, imagining the boardroom battles which must be made easier by that charisma. Reluctantly she had to admit that he seemed unaware of using it, although he must know that he possessed it. He seemed genuinely interested in his hosts and their life; the fact that the inordinately good-looking face hid a brilliant, incisive brain helped, too.

Afterwards they sat in the sitting room with only one lamp on and talked of everything until Elaine gasped and broke it up.

'Because Stephanie still wakes at five in the morning,' she excused herself, smiling, obviously regretful.

At her bedroom door Donald said to his daughter. 'Time we caught some more sprats for the cats. Shall I get you up when the baby wakes?'

She nodded, smiling in her turn. This was a ritual she remembered from the golden days of her childhood, the slow row out in the dinghy, paying the net out as she went and then the jump into the water which was always just too deep for her, to help her father pull the ends together. About the rest of it, the removal of the haul of small silver fishes, she preferred not to think, salving her conscience with the thought that Nature was cruelly severe. At least none of them was wasted.

CHAPTER FIVE

IN the grey dawn it was the thought of that deepish water which persuaded Christabel to put on her bikini with a woollen jersey pulled on over it.

Softly, so as not to wake their guest, she and Donald made their way through the house and down the track to the boatshed. One of the dogs lifted his head from his paws and whined softly against the rattle of his chain.

'Quiet, Joe!' Donald commanded sternly.

'Can't he come?'

He grinned. 'You know what he does when the net gets to the beach. Elaine will just have got off to sleep again and she won't like being woken up by a fusillade of barking.'

'Poor old Joe,' Christabel commiserated, listening as his tail thumped a couple of times. 'Does Elaine go back to sleep? She's always up at six-thirty.'

'Well, she says she doesn't, but she gives a pretty good imitation of it.' Donald cocked a weather eye at the rapidly lightening sky. 'Another fine day. We could do with rain.'

'Oh, you farmers! You're never satisfied!' Christabel linked her arm in his, listened with delight to his quiet chuckle.

The boatshed was nestled in under a low cliff, so overhung by enormous pohutukawas that it was barely visible. Even the blotched green paint, which her father had for years been threatening to replace, helped camouflage it. From it a jetty ran out, smaller than the collapsed one whose stubborn old piles could still be seen. In the old days the big jetty had been vital to the station; now the wool clip and cattle went by road and only pleasure boats came to Rangitatau.

On the still grey water the runabout sat cheeky in scarlet and white. A little further out was the launch, its outriggers proclaiming that it was used for deep-sea fishing, its fine, graceful lines an indication of its value. It was Donald Grieves' one extravagance.

Suddenly, so suddenly that it came as a shock, the sun leaped above the southern Gate; the sky turned from pale pink to gold and rose and the morning clouds began to dissipate.

For the first time in months Christabel was pierced by a pang of delight, so keen and sharp that it was almost a pain. Her lovely, husky laughter floated on the air. In the boathouse Donald Grieves heard the soft sound and gave silent thanks.

'O.K.,' he said laconically, sliding the dinghy down over the sand into the water. 'Take it easy now.'

Silently the oars moved through the water, silently the little boat described a semi-circle in the bay, the dark net drifting behind it. Up to his knees in water, Donald held one end of the net upright. When it was time Christabel shipped the oars and jumped out, grabbing her end of the net as she and her father ran side by side up on to the beach.

'Not a bad haul,' Donald observed with satisfaction. 'Leave it now, I know you hate this part. Go and get the dinghy.'

Beneath the discarded jersey Christabel wore an old shirt, unbuttoned, the tails tied in a tight knot beneath her breasts. It was too much bother to take it off, so she plunged straight into the refreshing coldness of the water, striking out strongly to where the dinghy drifted offshore. Fortunately it was a heavy old clinker-built so that when she hauled herself in over the side it rocked but kept right way up.

'What's the water like?'

'Super!' Christabel spoke over her shoulder as she brought the dinghy in. 'Like warm milk!'

It was an old joke and Donald answered as he always

had since she had discovered the phrase many years ago. 'Who'd want to swim in warm milk, for heaven's sake! There, that's done.' He put the two plastic buckets farther up the beach and began to pull the net together. 'Here, you take the net back to the boatshed. I'll put these in the freezer.'

The net smelled strongly of salt. At the boatshed Christabel hosed it carefully down with fresh water before draping it over a branch to dry. Then she hauled the dinghy up on to the sand and decided, after a glance at the sea now warming in colour, that she might as well work up an appetite for breakfast.

On the jetty she hauled off the shirt and did a model's strut along the cool, rough planks, holding a pose for some seconds before falling over the edge in a manoeuvre she had perfected at the age of eight.

The water hadn't had time to warm up, but this time she was ready for the shock, and came up gasping and triumphant, pushing her hair back.

To stare straight into Alex's angry face, the dark eyes like wet slate, cold and flat above a mouth thinned into a straight cruel line.

'Oh!' She could not stop herself, she covered her face with her hands, turning away as if he accused her of unnameable crimes. He had seen that stupid piece of play-acting and that remorselessly logical brain had made the connection.

But even as she arched backwards in rejection he grabbed her shoulders and shook her, his fingers tightening on to the smooth skin, pressing it painfully on to the fragile bones beneath.

'I thought you'd fallen,' he said harshly, and when she stared at him, unable to realise that she was reprieved, '*Kirsty*, don't look like that! I'm sorry I frightened you, but I thought you'd fallen and not come up again.'

'Oh.' Uncertainly she bit her lip. 'I—I swam underwater. I've very good——'

'Lung capacity,' he finished grimly. 'You don't have to tell me—I had you drowned!'

So he hadn't realised. Confidence flowed through her and she smiled, mischief bringing colour to her pale face. 'Oh, you can't drown a Grieves,' she said pertly. 'We're half mermaid, didn't you know?'

Instantly mockery leapt into his face. 'Mermaid? Siren, more like,' he said with soft emphasis, his bold gaze moving over her face and shoulders. 'I think you could lure any man to his death when you look like that.'

The colour in her cheeks deepened to a flush. 'Oh, you're an awful flirt,' she said, striving to be the ingenuous country girl he obviously thought her.

And twisted free of his relaxed grip; dolphin-like she curved into the water to come up again some yards away, that smile still caught at the corner of her lips while beneath it her brain worked furiously. Was he really unable to resist any reasonably personable woman, or did the sizzling electricity of their first encounter still hold true?

For herself she didn't know. Yesterday the shock of his appearance had robbed her body of any response but the sickening effects of panic. But just then, almost naked in his grip, she had felt the quick, gunpowder fizz in her blood which had presaged such disaster before.

Not again, she vowed, watching as he struck out across the bay, not ever again, no matter how strong the attraction. Once was enough to be burned so severely that the scars would be left on her personality for life. No, if he showed any inclination to flirt with her, somehow she must make it clear that she had no intention of succumbing. Briefly she considered stringing him along, indulging in a playful makebelieve flirtation, and just as quickly rejected it. She had not the self-control necessary for that sort of game.

Besides, she doubted very much whether any involvement with him could be other than intense.

Apart from her own reactions his had revealed that he was a man of strong passions. Oh, there was restraint too, an iron command of those passions, but she doubted very much whether he thought of women as anything other than legitimate prey.

Not virgins, however; she would just have to project a kind of rural innocence, she thought, narrowing her eyes to watch him against the sun. The glowing light sent scintillations of colour across her lashes. Normally she would have thought a vision of rainbows a good omen. Which just showed how stupid superstition was, she thought cynically, finally locating the dark head. Naturally he swam with skill and style, strong arms pulling his lean, shining body through the water with speed and an impression of well-contained power.

'Oh, go to hell!' she exclaimed on a sob as she turned away to swim back to the jetty.

The steps were cool, still damp with dew, although a faint mist rising from them revealed how efficient the newborn sun was at drying. Christabel pushed her hair back from her face and tilted her head, shaking water from one ear. Then she picked up her shirt and tied it back on, wishing fervently that she had at least worn one with buttons. If Alex was going to make a habit of appearing when least expected she would have to make sure she was adequately covered.

Oh, how she wished that the god in charge of coincidences hadn't decided to give things a stir yesterday! With Alex's arrival all the peace that Rangitatau represented had fled and she doubted very much whether it would ever again be the refuge she had made it. By keeping the two parts of her life totally separate she had managed to banish the Christabel who had behaved so stupidly in Australia, sinking gratefully into her Kirsty personality.

Alex's arrival somehow made that no longer possible. Willy-nilly she was forced to accept the Christabel side of her and it hurt and confused her.

Impatiently she turned to walk down the jetty to the house. Before she was halfway there he caught her up, a towel draped over his shoulder, big and virile with a faint arrowing of dark hair over his chest and down to meet the band of his bathing suit. He did not go in for the skimpy, skin-tight briefs worn by so many men, even those who were overweight and looked repulsive.

He wouldn't, of course. He needed no artificial emphasis of his virility. It was there, a part of him, as obvious as his good looks and as potent.

When he looked at her the speculation she had resented was gone from his expression, leaving a teasing good humour that surprised and bewildered her.

It lasted. Almost, as the days sped past, Christabel wondered if Rangitatau possessed some magic of its own, for the ruthless businessman seemed to have been left behind. Every night Alex made a collect call to Auckland, speaking for half an hour or so, but that was the sum total of his business activities. Apparently the Thomassin empire could function without him if necessary. It helped, of course, that Elaine had no idea who he was. About her father Christabel wasn't too sure. Donald was too widely read not to recognise the name, but if he did he certainly didn't give any indication of it. But Elaine treated him with her usual smiling friendliness, taking it for granted that he should be interested in the same things as they, that he should help Donald on the station and her in the house when it was appropriate.

'He keeps his room immaculately,' she reported with some satisfaction. 'The bed is always made and his clothes are not left lying around. All I have to do is dust!'

Christabel, who organised things so that she never had to go into the bedroom where he slept, nodded. 'Good for him,' she said, allowing indifference to colour her tones. 'Are you really going out to the lily pond tomorrow?'

'Yes, Donald says the waterlilies will be over soon and I haven't had a chance to see them this year. Why, don't you want to go?'

Most emphatically she did not, but she could not tell Elaine that. 'It's a long way,' she said. 'I thought it might be a bit much for Stephanie.'

'It's not when they're that age that they're difficult,' Elaine informed her. 'We'll have the carry-cot and a plentiful supply of nappies and a mosquito net, and Stephanie will be fine. If anyone feels it it will be Scott. He's quite determined to ride, you know.'

Like her brother Christabel had been put on a pony before she could walk and could remember just such expeditions in her childhood and her fierce determination to keep up with the adults.

'Oh, he'll manage,' she said, smiling. 'And if he starts to nod off—well, he can always ride with one of us. Would you rather I came in the Land Rover with you?'

'No, don't be silly!' Elaine looked arch. 'As if I'd deprive you of a chance to shine in front of Alex!'

It had to be said. 'Now, *don't* try any match-making!' Christabel was relieved to hear the laughing note in her voice and made her expression follow suit. 'He's a flirt, but he'd be the first to pull back if one of his partners got serious. Men like Alex marry in their own circles.'

'He doesn't strike me as a flirt,' Elaine mused, serious. 'Very charming and a bit of a tease, but flirt is too lightweight. As for marriage—well, what circle is his?'

'Very rich, the kind of wealth that's been in the family for generations.'

'Your father is not exactly poor.'

Christabel smiled and hugged her stepmother's thin shoulders affectionately. 'You're a darling to the bottom of your egalitarian little soul, and I love you, but let's put it this way. I know King Cophetua married the beggarmaid, but do you think his relations and friends welcomed her? Or that after the initial excitement she was happy in that great stuffy palace?'

Elaine could look remarkably stubborn when she wanted to. 'I think you suffer from an inverted form of snobbery,' she declared robustly, even as she flushed at Christabel's affectionate compliment, 'because there's not a—a circle anywhere you wouldn't grace. You're lovely-looking, you're as bright as a button and you're not afraid of work. More to the point, you have a kind, compassionate *loving* heart.'

And she turned away to hide the sudden tears in her eyes.

'Oh, lord, don't be like that,' said Christabel in an odd, wobbly voice. 'I mean, we've just got you back on your feet. Dad is going to be furious if you have red eyes when he comes in. He'll immediately banish the wicked stepdaughter.'

'It's the stepmother who's wicked, idiot.' But Elaine had regained control. 'And I know you hate thanks, but neither Donald nor I will ever forget just how much of a stalwart you've been these last months. Now,' with a return to briskness, 'let's decide what we're going to take to eat tomorrow. Peaches and melon and apples for fruit, I thought, and the left-over terrine of chicken and veal, as well as that delectable bread you bake. What else?'

'How about cold mutton and salads? If it's fine we won't need anything hot.'

It was fine, but just in case the weather turned chilly Elaine packed thermoses of soup as well as everything else. And Scott got his way, trekking off triumphantly on his own small, sturdy pony, a hat on his head and jeans covering his brown legs.

The lily pond was up in the hills. Long years ago, before the pines had been planted, it had been scooped out to use as a reservoir. Exactly who had introduced the first waterlily roots no one knew, although Christabel's grandmother was universally suspected, but they certainly found conditions to their liking. Every spring the round green leaves spread across the still, smooth waters, and through summer white, scented cups were lifted high to the sun. It was a charming touch of exoticism to the workaday station, and a favourite place with them all.

The way there was pleasant, at first across wide, smiling paddocks, then, as the sun grew hotter, they took to the firebreaks between the pines and rode in quietness with fantails darting between them, tails flirting as they snapped up insects disturbed by their passing.

Scott was so determined to stay the distance that he was silent most of the time, concentrating, but the other three rode with companionable conversation. Not for the first time Christabel found herself thinking how— well, it was a strange word to apply to Alex, but he could be just plain *nice*. Amusing, sometimes provocative, with a breadth of knowledge and interest which kept her brain at full stretch, and then, just pleasantly, companionably silent.

She and he embarked on a discussion about their favourite composers while Donald and Scott dropped back a little. It was very warm and still, for no breeze found its way between the sombre pines. Beneath the trees ferns grew luxuriantly, low, ground-hugging species and pongas which reached for the sky on long, rough black trunks. Periodically dragonflies zipped past, the enormous ones erroneously called horse-stingers as well as their smaller cousins the damselflies, vivid blue and red, their wings vibrating with urgency.

Behind and to the side three dogs foraged almost noiselessly, their tongues hanging as they explored, bright, intelligent eyes alert. Once one put up a pheasant which flew screaming into the depths of the pines. Three pairs of canine eyes fixed with desperate pleading on Donald.

'Get in behind,' he commanded, and they obeyed,

although the oldest showed what he thought of the decision by turning his back on the riders and scratching himself with vigour.

Christabel laughed softly, looked up to meet Alex's glance, as slyly amused as she was. A sudden upwelling of joy rendered her almost ecstatic.

'They say dogs are slavishly dependent,' she said to break the spell, 'but nobody's ever told Joe that!'

'This life obviously suits you,' Alex observed elliptically. 'Don't you ever want to get out into the world and do something else?'

'Not on days like this.'

'But on other days?'

Her expression firmed. Her mount flung up his head and cocked an ear back towards her. Perhaps some of her nervousness was communicating itself to him.

'Oh, everyone gets sick of things,' she parried, deliberately evasive. 'Don't you?'

'Yes, of course.' The bland voice hardened. 'But I'm in a job that uses every talent and aptitude I possess, that stretches me to the utmost and then some.'

'And I'm not?'

The wide shoulders moved in the smallest of shrugs, but his gaze held hers, demanding an end to her evasiveness.

'Yes, if you were like Elaine, finding complete fulfilment in her home and her family. But however devoted to them all you are, and your devotion is obvious, they're not your family, are they? Nor is this going to be your home for ever.'

Christabel half-turned in the saddle, pushing her hat back from her suddenly damp forehead. Donald and Scott had stopped but were slowly catching them up, Scott's high treble effectively giving Alex privacy for his probing questions.

'I'll cross that bridge when I come to it,' she said, twisting back to face the front. She stared stonily through her horse's ears, determined not to look at him.

She was tense, her skin prickling under the merciless scrutiny he fixed on her.

'In other words, you refuse to face it now.'

Anger glittered beneath her lashes. 'I don't think it's any business of yours,' she said deliberately, 'but I could marry in the district.'

'Ah, yes, the estimable vet.'

There was a note in his voice that she couldn't discern, and the set of his features gave nothing away as she darted a swift sideways glance at him.

After a moment he resumed, 'Elaine has mentioned him. On holiday, isn't he? Climbing mountains.'

Something in his voice invested the climbing of mountains with an immense foolishness.

Stung, she answered more fiercely than was wise, 'Yes, he is. A perfectly respectable hobby. Even rather courageous of him, I think.'

'People who need to test their mettle time and time again have a basic core of insecurity,' Alex countered smoothly. And as she turned indignantly towards him he laughed and flung up an indolent hand. 'No, don't say whatever it is that's trembling on your tongue. I know, because I used to race cars. At first it was to prove that I had the courage. Later I enjoyed it as a sport, but the basic need to test myself was always there. When I realised what I was doing I gave it up.'

'Why?'

'Because I knew myself a little better by that time.'

Christabel had been angry with his contemptuous dismissal of Nate's motives, but curiosity and the hidden desire to know more of him overrode it.

'So?' she said daringly.

He sent her a brief, hard smile. 'I no longer felt any desire—or need—to test my courage.'

'So the insecurity is gone.'

He flicked her a taunting, teasing smile, knowledge-able and worldly. 'Is it ever? Right at the core of every soul is the baby we were born as, craving the all-embracing protection that only our mother gave us. As we grow we think we may find the same kind of self-less, wholehearted love from a member of the opposite sex. Maturity is when we face the fact that it's gone, that it will never be repeated. All that we can hope for is a loving companion, a friendly lover, and God knows, that's rarely enough come by.'

'Oh,' she sighed, appalled, 'you're a complete cynic! Don't you believe in love at all?'

'Quickened heartbeats, the blood rushing through veins like fire—oh, I believe in that.' He sounded madly sophisticated, his words relegating her dreams to adolescent delusions. 'But that's not love, my sweet siren.'

So swiftly that she hadn't time to move he leaned over and clasped her wrist, lean brown fingers lying against the little pulsing beat there. Brilliant eyes caught hers and he smiled as the small traitor accelerated.

'And intellectual companionship, I understand that, too,' he said softly, releasing her to nudge his mount a sensible distance away. 'But that's not what you mean by love, is it? What you want is a mixture of Elizabeth Barrett Browning and John Donne.

"Whatever dies, was not mixed equally;
If our two loves be one, or thou and I
Love so alike, that none do slacken, none can die."'

He spoke the beautiful words beautifully, his voice so at variance with the mockery which made his face pagan that Christabel couldn't bear to look at him. And he had not finished. With the accuracy of a sharp-shooter he continued with that most famous of Elizabeth Barrett Browning's love poems:

'"I love thee to the depth and breadth and height
My soul can reach."

'Romantic claptrap, Kirsty. Insubstantial food for brains starved of reality. I don't understand that.'

For some reason the cool disdain in his tone hurt.

Forcing a smile into her voice, she countered lightly. 'You remind me of George Granville:

'Love is begot by fancy, bred
By ignorance, by expectation fed,
Destroyed by knowledge, and, at best,
Lost in the moment 'tis possessed."'

From behind her father said, 'Quoting poetry at each other, you two?'

And Scott, darling Scott, begged urgently, 'Tell me one, Kirsty. Tell me "This Old Man!"'

'No, you have to clap that one and I don't think the horses would like that! How about the one about the bear and the mountain?'

Scott insisted on them all singing it. To Christabel's surprise Alex joined in, imperturbable, his voice a pleasant baritone and the song obviously known to him. Clearly he numbered small children amongst his acquaintance. She found herself wondering if he had other family beside his sister, and then, with a sense of shock, whether Greg and Felicity were married yet.

It was the first time she had thought of them. Looking back, she found it difficult to recall the anguish she had felt at Greg's betrayal. As she sang, and kept on singing to encourage Scott's flagging energy, she wondered sardonically whether Alex had provided the money and expertise Greg had wanted for his business.

Of them all Fliss seemed to have come out of it worst, married to a fortune-seeker. She had looked interesting; a little haughty and reserved, but not arrogant like her brother or greedy like Greg. Perhaps Alex would mention them, although he hadn't referred to his family or his background at all since he had come to Rangitatau.

When they arrived at the pool the Land Rover was already parked in the shade and the rugs spread out, mostly in the shelter of the trees, but one had been left in the sun for anyone who wanted to sunbathe. In shorts and a suntop Elaine was playing with Stephanie, her back against the smooth bole of a kowhai tree. As she saw them she waved, finished the game and brought the baby across to the pool, watching as they rode their mounts into the cool water to let them drink.

'Have a good ride?' she asked as the horses blew daintily at the surface of the water. 'Ready for a drink yet?'

'I am,' Scott said stoutly, 'but when I've helped Daddy with mine horse.'

'Of course, darling.'

It was almost lunchtime. While the men saw to the horses Elaine and Christabel began to set out the food.

'Because you'll have to start back quite early,' Elaine explained. 'Scott will need to sleep before you go, or he'll never make it back.'

'He was good all the way here, stuck to it like a little trooper,' Christabel told her as she washed her hands and face in the pool.

'He's got plenty of go.' Elaine placed the baby on to the rug and handed her a scarlet rattle which Stephanie immediately waved languidly about. 'The first time Donald wanted to put him up on a horse I nearly had a fit, but I must admit now that it's a good idea. He told me that you'd learned to ride and swim before you could walk.' She smiled rather consciously, 'Of course, I couldn't have my children beaten by you! Horrid reasoning, wasn't it, but it did the trick.'

'I'm sure Dad wasn't trying to—to set one—no, that's not right. To compare us.'

'Of course not. He was just pointing out that living in a place like Rangitatau children need to be able to take care of themselves as much as possible. He was right, of course. It's one of his least endearing characteristics.'

Christabel laughed, the warm husky sound seductive

on the warm heavy air. 'Yes, even the best of men can sometimes prove right,' she teased, then ducked as Elaine threw an apple past her head.

'You just wait till you get married,' her stepmother threatened. 'You'll find there's nothing more irritating. Can you pull the chilly bin out of the Rover? It's underneath the bathing suits and towels.'

CHAPTER SIX

NEVER had food tasted better, eaten with a keen appetite beside the magic of the pool, its smooth surface ruffled by the exquisite cup-shaped blooms, every so often a wave of delicate perfume sent their way by a tiny breeze.

After the last peach had been eaten, the wine bottle drained and coffee drunk, Scott was discovered fast asleep on one corner of a rug, and Stephanie showed signs of wanting nourishment.

'Come and show me your pool.' said Alex, getting to his feet and holding out a hand to Christabel. Which was very nice of him since it meant that Elaine could nurse her daughter without moving away.

Christabel would have liked to join Scott in slumber. The lazy, drowsy, murmurous ambience was eminently conducive to dozing. However, she accepted the help Alex's hand offered, even suffering her fingers to lie resistless in his as they made their way through the grass to where the lilies met tangled grass in a haze of creamy blossom.

'An exotic scene,' Alex said abruptly, the arrogant head swinging as he took it in. In the sun the red highlights in his hair gleamed like dark fire. 'Pine trees with three ferns and fantails, a lily pond which could be traced back to Monet and the call of a bellbird mixed with a pheasant's honking.'

'That's a tui, actually,' Christabel told him. 'Look, you can see him up in the kowhai tree—he's the one with the blue-green sheen and the tuft of white feathers at his throat. We don't get bellbirds up here, unfortunately.'

'Any fish in the pond?'

She shook her head. 'No, not unless you count the little native ones, and no doubt there are plenty of eels.'

'Yet you swim in it?'

'Not in the pool itself. Up here.'

Just above the pool was another, smaller and without the lilies so that the sandy bottom could be clearly seen. It was about the size of a family swimming pool, almost circular in shape, murmurous with the sound of the stream that fed it, rippling and chuckling through a narrow little gully heavily shaded with one of the few remnants of native bush left.

'It looks cold,' Alex commented.

Christabel laughed softly up at him, her glance teasing. 'There speaks the soft Australian! We New Zealanders are made of much tougher fibre.'

'Think so?' A challenging gleam lit his narrowed smile. 'Let's see, shall we?' he murmured, and scooped her up, holding her out over the edge.

She laughed, 'You—you drop me and I'll—I'll——!'

'What will you do?'

It was just horseplay, he wouldn't be so, so *juvenile* as to drop her in! Yet although there was laughter in the tanned face so close to hers there was purpose too.

'I'll make sure you come in with me,' she threatened softly, aware of subtle signals from her body that told her she was in danger, that dumping her in the cool water would probably be the best thing to happen to her.

'Oh, in that case——!' And he turned so that she was once more safely over the ground. 'But I think I should demand a forfeit,' he said.

Even before he lowered his head she knew what his intention was, but her stupid mind couldn't get the right signals to her body fast enough, and she let him kiss her, bracing herself for the onslaught.

Only it wasn't. His mouth was warm and gentle, lingering on the silken softness of hers as though he loved the touch of it. Somehow her arms had found their way around his neck, probably when she had threatened to take him into the pool with her. Now they relaxed and the hands which had been tightly linked together opened and began to slide up into the crisp thickness of his hair, shaping the back of his head.

Against her mouth he made a funny little sound, almost a contented grunt, so that laughter filled her blood, bubbling through her like champagne, and he was smiling too as he lifted his head a fraction and gave her a long, enigmatic look, the brilliant eyes hooded, unrevealing.

Colour touched her skin with warmth, a glow which made her suddenly vulnerable and more beautiful.

'This,' he said deliberately, 'is all very well, but man is not made to carry big girls like you for too long.' And he showed just how strong he was by dropping to one knee and laying her on the ground, gently almost as though giving her the chance to stop this flirtation.

For that was all that it was, for both of them. A combination of the languidly beautiful surroundings, two people whose attraction for each other was almost purely physical, the pleasures of the table and a good wine—the whole drowsily sensuous atmosphere.

Common sense told her to roll away from beneath his kneeling form. Slowly she extended her hand and with her forefinger traced a line from his wrist to his elbow, her expression absorbed as though she was soaking in the feel of him, the long strength of his foreams, tangle of hair dark against the tanned skin, the lean elegance. Beneath her lashes her eyes were dreamy, soft with a promise she didn't understand.

She heard the swift intake of breath and then he was beside her, supporting himself on his elbow while his mouth travelled the contours of her face in tantalising little kisses. Sunlight soaked through her, the warm scent of crushed grass filling her nostrils. Deep in her bones there sprang into being an aching longing. She sighed, her lashes flickering, and touched him gently, measuring the width of his shoulders, her fingers stroking with wondering pleasure the flexed muscles beneath his shirt.

The muted thunder of his heart was an excitement in itself, fuelling the racing of her own. And then, suddenly, as his mouth reached hers, things changed, and she groaned, drowned in a shattering flood of desire that tensed her whole body, shaking it.

Instantly the hands on her shoulders gripped. Alex's mouth demanded surrender and she, lost in that fatal excitement, gave it to him, parting her lips so that he was able to explore the sweetness within. Across his back her hands clenched, pulling him down to her, every instinct urging her towards the only thing that would satisfy the hunger so swiftly, angrily aroused.

One of his arms slipped beneath her back, lifting her closer to that avid mouth which left her lips and traced the arched length of her throat. When it met the thin cotton of her shirt he muttered something but did not stop; even through the material she could feel the hunger in his mouth and when the burning throbbing bud at the centre of her breast was covered she gasped, her whole body arching against him in an agony of need.

His hand came up, unbuttoned her shirt; his mouth followed the path until it reached the fragile bra. It was when his finger probed beneath the pale cotton that she realised what her abandoned reaction to his lovemaking was leading to.

'No,' she whispered through lips which were swollen and slow. 'No, Alex—please!'

His hand moved to cover her breast, his thumb stroking across the taut tip, signaller of her arousal— and then he left her, and she twisted away, breath sobbing in her lungs, her head downbent in bitter humiliation as she refastened her shirt and tucked it back into the shorts she had donned as soon as they arrived.

When she summoned up the courage to turn around

he was sitting with his arms on his knees, head between them, hunched shoulders rising and falling to the depths of his breathing.

It gave her an acid pleasure to see just how strongly she affected him, pleasure mixed with shame. Whatever this—this *thing* between them, Alex felt it too, this dark tide of desire which so frightened her because she could not control it. It was as though the touch of his mouth was some kind of black enchantment, stripping her of principles and pride, leaving behind only frustrated passion, a body that craved his with all of the anguish of an addict.

He lifted his head, caught her angry, green stare, and smiled, twisted and sardonic.

'You pack a pretty lethal charge,' he observed, obviously trying to ease the hot sexual tension which thrummed between them. 'Shall we decide not to do that again? I doubt very much if I could stop next time, if there happens to be a next time, and I don't really want to explain to Donald that although I seduced his daughter she was every bit as enthusiastic as I.'

Christabel's anger collapsed, leaving her cold and hollow, still aching with need yet obscurely warmed by the fact that he had managed to leave her with some tatters of pride intact.

She managed to summon a smile. 'No, I doubt if he'd believe you,' she said, and shivered suddenly, realising how close they had been to discovery. Above the chattering of the stream her father's voice was lifted; a moment later he came up the small grassy bank that separated the two pools, the only protection a screen of kowhai trees, slender and insubstantial enough!

Thank God she and Alex were sitting a decent distance apart instead of lying locked together in an embrace which could have only one meaning! Donald was a modern and up-to-date farmer, but he had no time for the permissive morality. Not that he condemned those who fell from grace, he was too compassionate for that, but she had often enough heard the contempt in his voice at the antics of some pop or film star.

To be sure, his gaze swept them both with a sharp question which made her quiver inside, but he said merely, 'Scott's awake, so we might as well go for a quick exploration, if that's what you want to do.'

Christabel scrambled to her feet, her voice falsely bright, even to her own ears. 'Yes, let's.'

The day was spoiled. Yet nothing changed, not even Alex's attitude towards her. He was still the pleasant, teasing commpanion he had been, treating her as if she was a charming friend of his sister's, with just enough awareness to spice the relationship but not spil it.

She did her best to reciprocate, but in spite of the warning in his gaze was unable to prevent a certain wary stiffness whenever he came near.

Until he said, quite softly as they were halfway home and Donald had moved away a little with Scott, 'Your father is almost certain to think I've made a pass at you and been rudely turned down.'

And because it was impossible to credit such an unlikely assertion she laughed, aware of the caustic note in the sound but hoping that Donald, at least, wouldn't notice it.

'That's better,' Alex encouraged, the clear-cut lines and planes of his face totally without expression except for a leaping mockery in the brilliant eyes.

And that, incredibly, was that. In subsequent days the incident was not mentioned between them again. Once more Christabel began the wearisome task of burying it deep in her subconscious, blotting it out as she had tried to blot out that catastrophic first meeting. In this she was helped by Alex, who was so—so *friendly* that even through her bewilderment she found herself relaxing in his presence.

Almost she could delude herself into thinking again that his physical presence meant nothing to her. Then, when she wasn't expecting it, she would see him from the corner of her eye, and her body would be flooded with a heated hunger, overwhelming, almost irresistible.

But she was able to resist it. Nate's return helped. The night he arrived back he took her to dinner in the nearest town of any size, twenty miles away up the coast, so she was forced to introduce them, the man who had taken her virginity—no, who had just taken up an offer, she thought grimly—and the one who treated her with tenderness and respect as though she was still all innocence.

For some reason she half expected Alex to be up when she arrived back, tired and yawning, just before midnight, but apart from the light Elaine always left on on the big porch which held gumboots and raincoats the house was dark. And silent as the grave. And cold. Outside the sky was blazing with the jewels of the night, but the beauty of it left her without emotion, she who had always thrilled to beauty.

Shivering, she undressed and got into bed, so cold that after ten minutes she leant over and switched the electric blanket on.

And, of course woke up three hours later dripping with perspiration.

Altogether, a frustrating night, especially as Nate had told her that he was leaving the next day for a course in Whangarei, which meant that she would have to go to a party at the Muirheads' place without him.

'Why have a party in the middle of the week?' Elaine asked when Christabel told her the next morning as she was ladling out Scott's porridge.

Turning down the element beneath the pan of bacon, Christabel answered, 'Oh, it's Rob's twenty-first birthday and she thinks birthdays should be celebrated on the correct day.'

'Heaven help those who have to turn up at work the next day!' Elaine lifted her voice slightly. 'Oh, Donald, Nate has to go away today, so can Kirsty have the car tomorrow night? You won't mind taking the ute for your wretched meeting, will you, darling?'

Christabel bit her lip. Her ears had recognised the sound of two men entering, and for some reason she didn't want Alex to hear that she was going to this party alone.

However, it was inevitable. In answer to Donald's query Elaine told him about Nate's course.

'Well, I suppose you'd better have the car, then,' Donald agreed, adding slyly. 'I can see it's all part of a plot to persuade me to buy another car. I don't know how long it is since I used this one! I'll have to check the points on the ute.'

'Well, why not borrow mine?' Alex's voice was cool and matter-of-fact.

There was a short silence. Christabel began to put bacon and two carefully cooked eggs on to the hot plates she had taken from the warmer.

'Better still, why don't you go to the Muirheads' party with Kirsty, Alex?' Elaine's voice was excited and pleased. 'It will be more fun for Kirsty to have a partner, and Ash and Rob would love to meet you. They're the most hospitable pair! And their parties are always fun, aren't they, Kirsty?'

Well, what could she say?

'Lovely,' she agreed woodenly, setting one plate before Donald and the other in front of Alex.

'I can hardly just barge in,' Alex said lightly, his eyes lingering on Christabel's flushed features before moving down to his meal.

'For heaven's sake, they won't mind in the least.' Elaine chuckled, her expression suddenly mischievous. 'As a matter of fact, you'll be doing Kirsty a good turn.'

'Oh, why?' Alex sounded amused.

Christabel stopped fussing with the breakfast and looked enquiringly at her stepmother.

'Because Penny Mountain is going to be there.

She's on holiday, which I think must mean between jobs.'

'Oh, *no!*' Christabel shuddered, remembering Penny Mountain. Especially the high, little-girl voice that never missed an opportunity to point out Christabel's shortcomings and the round hard blue eyes that saw them all.

'Who,' Alex enquired with enjoyment, 'is Penny Mountain?'

Elaine chuckled, pouring out orange juice for Scott. 'Well, I believe it started at school. They became bosom enemies there, but on Penny's side at least, the years haven't healed a thing. Last time they met Penny made a determined attempt to inveigle Nate away from Kirsty and almost irritated Kirsty into losing her temper, something which is not easily done, I assure you.'

'She's a twit,' Christabel said briefly. 'I mean, for heaven's sake, so we didn't like each other at school and once I pushed her into the sheepdip! Well, she told the teacher I cheated in the spelling exam when all I was doing was reading a book! Not that Miss Prout believed her. But to carry on as if we're in the middle of a blood feud—she's a nutcase!'

'That fixes it,' Alex declared. 'I must meet this Penny Mountain. If you won't take me with you, Kirsty, I'll gatecrash.'

What else could she do? 'I'll ring up Rob Muirhead,' she said, trying to inject some lightness into her tones. 'Besides being a nutcase, Penny's very pretty. If you like dolls!'

Donald let out a quiet chuckle at the pointed comment and Alex grinned, that attraction so blatant that it made her heart leap within her breast.

Rob Muirhead was delighted at the thought of someone new at her party. 'Is he good-looking?' she asked in her quick way. Christabel let her glance wander to where Alex had just come into sight. 'Madly,' she said drily. 'Like a god. A Latin one, I think, dark and smouldering.'

The telephone she was using was the one in the hall. In the dimness she saw the flash of his smile and waited expectantly.

'Terrific!' Rob breathed. 'But more important, has he got character?'

Some devil impelled Christabel. Tipping her head to one side, she surveyed the now stationary figure before her and said thoughtfully, 'Oh, loads of it. Now, how can I describe him? Arrogant, I suppose, like the best romantic heroes. Mr Darcy rather than Mr Rochester, although——'

Her voice broke off into a squeak as, smiling, Alex bent his head and bit her earlobe, then holding her head still, explored the convolution within with the tip of his tongue.

When she could move she was brilliantly flushed, her eyes slumbrous and Rob was demanding, 'What's going on? Kirsty . . .?'

'Nothing,' she said, turning her back. A moment later she continued more firmly, 'Nothing at all, Rob. I was just—just taken by surprise, that's all.'

'Oh, that's all, is it?' Rob wasn't in the least appeased. 'What took you by surprise? Not the romantic hero. I hope?'

'No, no, of course not.'

He hadn't moved from behind her; in fact, with the skin on her back she could feel him only a few inches away. But when he drew her to rest against him and smoothed the cap of hair aside so that he could kiss the nape of her neck she lost all control of the situation.

'Look, I'll have to go now, Rob,' she gabbled. 'I'll see you tomorrow night, O.K.? Bye!'

And slamming the receiver down she whirled and lifted sparkling eyes to his. Although the light in the hall was dim she could see the taunting gleam beneath his lashes.

'Don't throw challenges my way,' he said softly, the mocking note in his voice entirely failing to hide the danger that lurked there. 'What else did you expect Kirsty? That I'd let you get away with it?'

Well, no. She knew him better than that. He hadn't got where he was by avoiding challenges, although he wasn't the stupidly foolhardy kind who ignored everything else in his eagerness to accept a dare. Very definitely, he was the kind whose head ruled every other aspect of character. But she doubted if he'd ever refused the kind of sexual provocation she had offered.

So she had deliberately goaded him, and he knew it. Shame tightened the skin across her cheekbones as she said in a stifled voice, 'No, I suppose not.'

But as she turned away he laughed quietly and caught her with gentle firmness by the elbow.

'Don't look so tragic,' he teased. 'I like the few instances I've seen of that rather quirky sense of humour. It comes flashing out when I'm least expecting it and then retreats, almost as if you're afraid. Are you, Kirsty?'

'Of you?' It was an effort to lighten her voice, but she did it, even gave a kind of half smile. 'No, not afraid.'

'But cautious. Even wary. What is it about me you don't like, Kirsty? And don't try to tell me there isn't something. I felt it beating against me the first time you saw me.' His hand moved slowly down to capture her wrist, his thumb resting gently against the pulse that beat there.

'I find you—intimidating,' she said carefully, looking down at their hands, the contrast between the olive tan of his skin, the pale gold of hers. For a man he was lean, not huge, yet against the deceptive fragility of hers his hand looked big, its strength leashed but ever present.

'Why?'

She shifted position uneasily, afraid of telling him too much but aware that he was too astute not to notice an evasion. 'You—you overwhelm me,' she muttered. 'I don't like it.'

'You are afraid. Not so much of me, but of what I represent.' His voice was cool and judicial, almost without emotion. As if to emphasise his lack of involvement he released her and leaned one shoulder against the time-dimmed kauri panelling, his eyes half-closed as they scanned her face.

'I don't know what you mean.' The words came out hurriedly, sounding almost breathless as though he had shocked her.

'Yes, you do. You're not stupid. Why do you shy from any sort of involvement?'

'For the same reason as you, I suppose,' she returned with spirit.

He smiled. 'Oh, I doubt it,' he said drily. 'You see, whether you admit it or not, you are involved, far more involved with me than with your handsome vet. No——' as she backed away, her expression set and angry, 'no, don't run away. You're rather good at that, but it's not going to get you anywhere. It never does. That was your mother's technique, wasn't it? She ran, ran from the life she disliked here, ran from any sort of emotional involvement—'

'You didn't know her,' Christabel snapped. 'And I'll bet nobody here has discussed her with you. Leave me alone! I don't need your pop psychology. Just because I haven't fallen flat on my face for you you think there must be something wrong with me! Well, for your information, you conceited egomaniac, my mother——'

His hand across her mouth cut short her tirade. Above the long fingers her eyes blazed green as emeralds.

'I think we should pursue this subject somewhere else,' Alex drawled, indicating with a jerk of his head that someone had moved in the front of the house.

'I don't want—I'm not—oh, *leave* me alone!'

But his hand on her arm was not to be denied. Willy-nilly it urged her along the hall and on to the front verandah, then down the steps and over the narrow path to the beach.

Once out of sight of the house she turned, hand raised.

'No, you little wildcat,' he said, almost lazily, catching the wrist and bringing it to his mouth so that the kiss was pressed on to her clawed fingers. 'You can use some of that superfluous energy by climbing.'

He more or less forced her up one of the steep hills which had been used by the old Maoris as a fortress. At the top was a levelled area. Sheep had grazed the turf very short so that it was like a small plateau with a magnificent view across Rangitatau and out through the Gates to the sheet of silver that was the Pacific Ocean.

'O.K., sit down,' Alex ordered, taking off his shirt to make a rug.

Mutinously Christabel sat on the grass instead, avoiding the sight of that wide brown torso looming above her.

'Kirsty!' he threatened gently, hands on narrow hips, long legs apart in the classic stance of a man about to make his presence felt.

'Oh, I've only got jeans on and they won't stain. Your shirt is good material, too good to cover in grass stains.' She spoke jerkily, pulling at an inoffensive tuft of grass with short, vicious movements.

He laughed and sat down beside her, too close for comfort, but although she willed him to do it he did not put his shirt back on.

'So,' he said deliberately. 'Your mother. She ran from Rangitatau because she couldn't take it any longer, the isolation and the lack of cultural stimulation.'

'You must remember that it was more difficult then,' she retorted in her mother's defence, tacitly giving him the right to discuss the subject. 'The roads aren't much today, but then they were ten times worse. There was no television and even radio reception was poor.

Sometimes she went for months without setting foot off the place.'

'I know.' Oddly he sounded almost sympathetic. 'It must have been hell for her, especially when she fell out of love with Donald. And he with her.'

Heat prickled between Christabel's shoulders, making her uncomfortable.

'Yes, well, I suppose so. I didn't know much about it. They—they never quarrelled in front of me, or anything.'

'No.'

A long pause, during which she rested her chin on her knees, staring moodily down into the rock pools at the base of the hill. In one large one a big snapper hung embedded in the translucence of the water. So small were the movements of tail and fins needed to keep it there that it seemed motionless, a silver shape set in jade and amethyst.

'And when you were in Australia, did she form any new attachments?' he asked almost casually.

Christabel's head came up with a jerk. Astounded, she stared into the implacable features above her. 'No!' she exclaimed.

'No lovers?'

'No!'

'So she ran from emotional involvement, too.' A cruel hand caught her wrist as she scrambled to her feet, jerked her from her feet and into a heap on top of him. He grunted as her body hit his, but held her there, effortlessly resisting her fight to get free.

At last, gasping and sore, she lay above him, trying desperately not to feel the hard length of his body beneath her. His grip relaxed but she knew better than to try and free herself.

'Mm,' he said, his eyes almost closed. 'You're afraid of entanglement too, aren't you, Kirsty? Afraid of any sort of commitment. That's why you go out with Whatsisname, who makes it quite clear that although he likes you he's not in the market for an affair. He's no threat to you.'

'And you think you are?' Her voice was hard with scorn. 'As I said before, you've colossal conceit, Alex Thomassin.'

'If you'd like to think that. I prefer to think of it as curiosity,' he returned smoothly.

'Curiosity? Just because you're *curious*—you put me on a pin and dissect me? Well, for your information——'

'How you do go on,' he complained gently, and shut her up by kissing her, firmly and extremely sensuously, until she was silenced and clung, while tears gathered on her lashes.

'That's why I'm curious,' he murmured, removing the glittering traitors with the tip of his tongue, his mouth warm against her heavy eyelids. 'Because I find you intensely attractive, my rather mysterious siren, so desirable that it's only my respect for your innocence and to a lesser extent, the fact that I'm a guest in your father's house plus an oddly old-fashioned streak in me which prevents me from seducing you. What's the matter, Kirsty?'

For his comment about her innocence had struck her like a blow to the heart. With an incoherent sound she stiffened in a revealing involuntary movement.

Instantly his hands captured her face, turning it up to his so that the hard eyes could read its pale contours.

'So that's it,' he said, and something flickered deep in his scrutiny. 'Redeeming yourself, are you, Kirsty? What happened? A fling followed by a year's penitence and hard work and denial of yourself and your needs? Are you a Puritan?'

How could he now know? Surely something of that night's laughter and passion had lingered in his subconscious if nowhere else. A kind of anguish closed her eyes as she trembled.

Instantly he let her go, his arms enfolding her in that most comforting of embraces while his cheek came to rest on the burnished cap of hair. Beneath her face the hard, slightly roughened wall of his chest rose and fell in a rhythm as old and as satisfying as the sea. The muted thunder of his heart filled her ears. She had never felt so safe, so secure, held captive in the arms of a man she barely knew, a man whose constant presence had become almost a necessity to her as well as a constant danger to her peace.

How long they lay like that she didn't know. But at last Alex said calmly, 'Much as I like this, my dear, we'd better get back before Elaine sends out a search party.'

And when she didn't answer he chuckled softly and sat up, holding her still while he stared down into her flushed, bemused face. 'You look about sixteen,' he said a little grimly. 'Such a graceful, secretive, frightened sixteen. Don't blink so guiltily, Kirsty. I'll wait until you want to tell me all about it.'

'There's nothing to tell you,' she said, coming out of the daze of pleasure into swift defiance.

He grinned as he got to his feet and hauled her upright. 'Oh yes,' he said with great certainty, the straight, satyr's brows twitched together. 'Confession is good for the soul, didn't you know?'

CHAPTER SEVEN

Just before they left for the Muirheads' party Alex astounded them all by telling them that he would be leaving the next morning.

At least, he astounded Elaine and Christabel, and upset Scott, who astounded them all over again by bursting into tears and having to be comforted by Alex with a promise to return soon.

'And stay?' Scott hiccupped, his pugnacious little face lifted adoringly to Alex.

'If I can,' said Alex.

The child's eyes filled with tears again and he clung to his hero's hand. 'For a holiday?'

Alex's expression was tender as he picked up his small worshipper and gave him a cuddle. 'My holiday's over,' he said gently, 'but I'll come back before I go home, I promise. How would you like to get a postcard from me, from Australia?'

It was a brainwave. 'With a koala on it?'

'Yes.'

Scott nodded eagerly and in the face of such a promise remained tearless even after being set back on his feet.

Incredible, but Alex Thomassin, who treated women like playthings, would be a good father when he finally felt the dynastic urge. Even the baby liked him and cooed happily in his arms, held securely and confidently. Perhaps he was used to children. Perhaps Fliss and Greg had a child.

On the way in Christabel said abruptly, 'You seem very confident with children. A doting uncle?'

'Not yet.' He sounded detached. 'My sister has been married once, but it didn't work out. She was going to try again last year, but that fell through; much to my relief she decided to wait and see if she could find a man she respected to be the father of her children.'

'I gather you didn't like her fiancé,' she said drily, thinking oh, poor Greg! All his bright dreams shattered.

There was an odd note in his voice as he answered. 'No. He was greedy, a grasping hypocrite with a strong eye to the main chance and a total lack of scruples.'

How right you are! Aloud she murmured, 'A scathing indictment. I conclude your sister was temporarily blinded by infatuation when she became engaged to him.'

'Suffering from shell-shock,' he said briefly. 'I think she realises now that in spite of everything she still needs her first husband.'

'Everything?' It didn't occur to Christabel that she was displaying an unwelcome curiosity. Nor did Alex seem to resent her interest.

The broad shoulders lifted in a slight movement. 'They married too young. Their desires outran their ability to cope with them. Not the best reason for marriage, but it might have worked out. Unfortunately Fliss's mother-in-law is one of the clinging, sweet-strychnine types. Fliss had no idea of how to deal with that sort of deliberate sabotage and her husband was too emotionally close to his mother to see what was happening.'

'And you?'

Alex shrugged again. 'I was busy, too busy to appreciate the situation until it was too late. Not that I could have done much. Sean has a considerable amount of pride—Fliss, too, for that matter. I think they'll get together again. Sean's mother rather overplayed her hand and he's awake to her potential for mischief now. All they have to do is overcome their pride.'

'All?'

He smiled in swift recognition of her disbelief. 'Well, it's been done before. Tell me, Kirsty, would you sink your pride for the man you wanted?'

'If I didn't it wouldn't be love, would it?' She was rather proud of the swift, almost laconic parry. It gave nothing away, admitted to nothing.

'So they say, all those poets who speak of love. Could you do it, Kirsty? Expose yourself nakedly to someone else's gaze, without the protection of that remote little mask you wear?'

Christabel shivered. 'I don't know,' she returned in an appalled voice. 'The idea frightens me.'

'Not only you. Is this the place?'

The fact that he had remembered where the Muirheads' letter box fronted on to the road should not have surprised her, since he was a man who noticed everything.

'Yes,' she said colourlessly.

Penny Mountain was there, her pretty doll's face expressionless as her round, thickly lashed eyes rested a moment on Christabel, but even Penny couldn't hide her interest in Christabel's escort. Being Penny, she didn't even try. A curious kind of confusion warred a moment with avidity in her expression. The avidity won and when Rob Muirhead, slightly dazed herself, introduced them Penny moved in for the kill.

'You're not local?' she asked breathlessly, ignoring Christabel.

'No, I'm an Australian. From Melbourne.'

'Oh.' Those round, pebbly eyes moved from his face in a graphic sweep over the expensive well-tailored clothes. 'How long are you staying?'

You wouldn't have guessed that beneath his superb manners there was amusement. Not unless you knew him very well. Which was strange, because Christabel recognised his hidden laughter and there was no way you could say that she knew him well.

'Unfortunately,' he said blandly, 'I have to leave tomorrow.'

Penny's round accusing gaze settled on Christabel's serene face. 'Nice for you, Kirsty. An old friend?'

Some devilish impulse made her say sweetly. 'No, but a good one, I hope.'

And Alex smiled down into her teasing eyes and agreed with smooth charm that they were good friends.

'As good as you and Nate?' Penny persisted, hammering home the point. 'Where is Nate, by the way?' She stared around as though expecting him to appear from out of the wallpaper.

'On a course,' Christabel murmured, then Rob moved them off to the next person she wanted Alex to meet and Penny was left behind.

Only for a short while. During the evening, and true to Elaine's expectations it went on until the early hours, Penny managed to make her presence felt. Everywhere Alex was, she appeared. Several times Christabel glanced across the room and saw them talking, but Alex was in too much demand for Penny to monopolise him. Not that he would have allowed such a thing to happen. Whatever else he was and had, he possessed the kind of ingrained courtesy which would have prevented such a monopoly. There would be few situations, social or otherwise, that would disturb his *sangfroid*.

The evening swirled past. At supper time Rob cut a beautifully iced cake, was toasted in champagne and made a short, humorous speech in thanks. Ash put on records and they danced to the smoky sweet sounds of Rob's favourites.

'Pure slush,' that forthright woman said cheerfully, 'but deliciously sentimental.' She eyed her party with a well-deserved complacency. 'Well, Kirsty, I think it's a howling success, don't you?'

Well, not exactly, no, but hers, Christabel was willing to admit, was a particularly biassed impression of the evening.

'You always give marvellous parties,' she replied, 'and this is better than most.'

'Thanks in no small part to your willingness to share that delectable man.' Rob eyed him with unfeigned interest. 'You know, I adore men with long legs and shoulders like lumberjacks'. Who is he? And I don't mean just his name. He's *someone*, you can tell. People don't acquire that effortless air of authority unless they use it a lot. Mind you, your Alex looks as though he was born with it.'

'He's not *my* Alex,' Christabel protested a little too sharply. 'He's up here on holiday, that's all.'

'And he doesn't fancy you? Come on, pull the other one! Poor old Penny's been doing her pocket Venus act all evening and he treats her with an exquisite courtesy which would freeze off anyone less thick-skinned than Penny, and watches you. Did you meet him in Australia?'

'*No!*' Christabel reacted to her hostess's sceptical words with a quick negative, before recovering her composure just a little too late. 'No, he just arrived up to have a look at the place, literally at the gate, and you know Dad and Elaine, they had him ensconced in the spare bedroom before he had a chance to say no.'

'I don't suppose he wanted to if he saw you first,' Rob said cheerfully. '*I* think he's gorgeous, and I'd be very surprised if he "just arrived". He doesn't look as though he's ever had an aimless thought or done anything without a reason in his life. Still, that's your story, my dear, don't let me put you off it.'

Sometimes Rob could be irritating, Christabel decided, usually because she had an uncanny knack of being correct. Not in this instance, however.

Then they were both claimed for a dance and she gave herself up to the friendly, casual conversation that was necessary, smiling her pleasure and interest, her expression warm yet always touched with a kind of serene remoteness which acted as a shield, a protection against too close a contact.

Until it was Alex who took her in his arms and for a moment the past and present coalesced into one and she looked up at him with eyes which gave away secrets.

Beside his beautifully moulded mouth a tiny muscle flicked, then tightened as though even that small betrayal was not allowed.

Faint colour warmed Christabel's fine skin, a pale wave which swept the long length of her throat and died on her cheekbones leaving her eyes like tired jewels. Yet she could not look away from his narrowed scrutiny, her glance caught and held in helpless subjection.

'You have eyes like aquamarines,' he remarked conversationally. 'Most of the time they're exactly halfway between blue and green, but when you're angry or afraid they intensify into green. And when I've kissed you into submission they gleam like the darkest sapphires.'

It was difficult to retain her composure in the face of such a determined assault, but although her colour deepened she forced herself to smile, even managed to infuse it with a certain sardonic appreciation.

'While your eyes remind me of wet slate,' she returned, proud of the crisp note in her voice. 'So dark that they're no colour, yet with a tinge of deepest green.'

Those straight brows lifted in dry amusement. 'If I gave you my child, I wonder what colour its eyes would be?' he mused, moving his hand so that it slid up her back over the gold georgette of her blouse.

For a moment her heart beat so loudly in her throat that she could not speak. Her colour ebbed and she lowered her gaze to where the fine silk of his shirt cut across his throat.

'A matter of genetics,' she said after a long nerve-tearing moment. 'Probably most undistinguished.'

'Mm. Red hair, I imagine. Yours has auburn highlights, and so has mine. Certainly any child we'd produce would be tall, and olive-skinned. I'm darker than you, but you're no pallid lily. Almost certainly good-looking, wouldn't you say?' There was laughter in his words, laughter with an underlying depth which made her heart race frantically in her breast.

'No comment?' he taunted, his breath erotic as it teased her ear. 'Would you like to bear my child, Kirsty? I'd enjoy giving you one.'

'Are you proposing, Alex?' Somehow, drawing on some deeply hidden reservoir of strength, Christabel made her voice alight with a rippling mockery, the face which lifted to meet his amused and candid. 'No? Then I'm afraid that any child must be purely—or impurely—hypothetical. You know, I'd have thought you more careful than that. Men your age don't usually go round putting themselves in a position where they might be misunderstood.'

He smiled down at her, irony and a kind of respect commingled. 'I'm quite capable of extricating myself from any position. If I asked you to marry me, what would you say?'

'No.'

His sigh was a theatrical flourish. 'Alas, you've dashed my hopes. I believe the correct thing to do now is leave abruptly and go big-game hunting in Africa for a year or so.'

So he'd been joking. Well, of course he'd been joking! And so had she. Then why did she feel as though he had thrown her over for another woman?

'Instead, you'll go back to Australia and hunt a different kind of big game,' she said lightly. 'Purely as a matter of interest, Alex, how can you run your sort of empire on a half-hour phone call each day? I thought tycoons lived for their business twenty-four hours a day.'

The wide shoulders moved, but he didn't look surprised at her tacit admission that she knew who—and what—he was.

'I delegate to people I trust. And I have an extremely good private secretary. But I'm not a freebooter, out cutting throats and swashbuckling. My kind of business is almost sedate. I enjoy it, otherwise I wouldn't do it, but I enjoy other things too. And I make sure that I find time to do those.'

'Like losing yourself in the backblocks.'

Those thick lashes hooded his eyes, but she felt the withdrawal in him, palpable, a kind of mental 'No Trespassing' sign.

'Oh, I never get lost,' he said lightly.

On the way home Christabel hoped, rather sadly, that he would kiss her before they went to their respective beds. Exactly what her emotions for him were she didn't know; total confusion was not exactly conducive to self-examination. But although he had promised to see Scott again, and she knew that he would keep his promise, she knew too that nothing would ever be the same. There was never any going back. The attraction between them was as strong as ever it had been, a deep, sensual flaring of need which overshadowed the fact that she had come to feel liking and respect for him.

Something perilously like love, in fact, and like love doomed to nothing, for he didn't believe in such a condition. Even when referring to his sister's marriage he hadn't used the word, not once. Needs, he'd said, respects, that was all. No mention of love.

She got her wish. At her door he held her and kissed her. His mouth was wonderfully tender, as though she was a loved friend, and when he released her and said 'Goodnight,' she couldn't respond because she was taut with frustration and desire and at that moment she hated him with every cell and core of her body.

He left early, almost immediately after breakfast, and the next day brought a parcel, posted in Whangarei, with gifts for them all—a book for Donald, a new one of exquisite photographs of birds, and for Elaine a flask of French perfume.

'Oh, he is *so* clever,' Elaine whispered rapturously, gingerly applying a tiny drop to her wrist. 'Smell it, Donald. It's *beautiful!*'

Her husband sniffed obligingly, then frowned. 'It is, but it's not your usual sort, is it? A little heavy?'

'It's exactly the sort of perfume I'd like to be the woman to wear.' Elaine laughed, then sighed. 'Cunning, far-sighted Alex. What has he sent you, Kirsty?'

'An aquamarine,' she said in a tight voice. 'Look.'

It was a ring, the exquisite deeply coloured stone not too large, in a modern setting of silver.

'Oh!' Elaine breathed, her glance flashing quickly from Christabel's set face to Donald's arrested one. 'Oh, how lovely!'

'He'll have to take it back,' Christabel said stonily. 'It's too much.'

'No, Kirsty—they're only semi-precious, surely.' Elaine appealed for help to her husband. 'Surely she can keep it, Donald?'

He said merely, 'Kirsty must do what she wishes, but I'd say that stones of that colour and clarity come expensive.'

'At least try it on, Elaine begged.

So reluctantly, as if even putting it on her finger was compromising her principles, Christabel slid it on to her finger. Of course it looked superb. Trust Alex to choose so well!

With a swift, ragged movement she pulled it off and set it back into its little black box, clicking the lid back to cover it with a kind of dull viciousness.

Scott was rapturous over the set of red and white plastic blocks which had arrived; there was an exquisitely made and smocked frock for Stephanie.

'I'd give a lot to see him buying that,' Elaine said wistfully, holding it in reverent hands. 'Do you think he got a woman to get it for him?'

'Alex?' In spite of herself Christabel couldn't prevent the hard note in her voice. 'No, Alex could cope with any situation. I can just see him setting the whole shop in a fluttering uproar until he found the one frock he liked for Stephanie.'

As Elaine chuckled and agreed Donald's gaze left his daughter's face, but that night he said quietly, out of Elaine's earshot, 'Do you know where to send the ring?'

'Yes.'

Thomassin Holdings had an office in Auckland. She could get the address from the telephone book and parcel up the wretched thing and send it there, marking it personal. It would cost the earth to insure it, but she wanted it out of her hands. When she had first laid eyes on the pretty, expensive bauble a kind of outrage had gripped her; it was there now, stifling her with its force. And she didn't really know why, unless it was because the whole thing smacked of a pay-off for services rendered.

'Did you read his letter?'

'Yes. Very prettily put.'

Donald frowned. 'Don't you think he meant it?'

'Oh, of course he meant it! You must have realised, Dad, that he was having a thoroughly good time here.'

'Well, I just say he fitted in very well. Apparently he has pastoral interests in Australia.' Donald picked up the newspaper, glanced casually at the headlines and set it down again, adding mildly, 'I must say I liked him. A hard man, but one I'd be disposed to trust.'

Christabel understood. 'Yes,' she said, trying to speak objectively, 'you'd meet few men more trustworthy.'

Her eyes met her father's steadily. After a moment Donald nodded and picked up the paper again.

It was easy enough to reassure her father. As she packed the beautiful ring Christabel found her eyes filling with tears. Angrily she dashed them away, for it was stupid to feel forlorn just because he had gone.

The next day was hot and breathless, no breeze stirring the trees or marring the bay. After lunch Cristabel took the Land Rover and drove into the village with the little parcel and a list of groceries. It was pleasant to meet people and catch up on the local gossip, but she felt that somehow the gloss had gone from her life.

'O.K.,' she said aloud on the way home, 'so you like him a lot, and he excites you. You're one of many, you fool. Forget him, because he's forgotten you already.'

Good advice. All she had to do was to learn to follow it.

Immediately she stepped into the house she knew that something was wrong. Her father and Elaine rarely argued, and their spats were short and swiftly forgotten, but Elaine had been crying and Donald's face was set in lines of rigid self-control. As Christabel looked from one to the other Elaine got up and hurried out of the room, head bent to hide the further onset of tears.

'What is it?' Christabel moved quickly to the big old table with the mail scattered across it. 'Has there been bad news?'

Her father hesitated, then pushed a sheet of paper across. 'Yes. You'd better read it for yourself.'

It was a letter from Auckland. A quick glance at the signature disclosed that it was written by Mr Panapa who had lived next door until forced to leave. In his old man's hand it set out the tribal Corporation's plans to develop their land at Rangitatau into a complex of hotels and motels and camping grounds.

The words danced before Christabel's horrified gaze. Pale, gnawing her bottom lip, she collapsed into a chair and re-read it again, from the beginning with its dignified assurance that had the writer not been confined to hospital he would have come to see his old friend himself to tell him the news, right through to the salutation at the end.

When the sheet of paper fluttered from her fingers she said quietly, 'They can't, can they? Daddy, they *mustn't!*' She hadn't called him that for years and it was a cry for reassurance.

He sighed and folded the letter up, then with a lack of purpose unusual in him unfolded it again, staring at it. 'Of course they can, Kirsty. It's their land. And don't think it hasn't taken them a considerable amount of thought to come to this decision. They love Rangitatau even more than we do, if that's possible.'

'Then why destroy it?' she cried hotly, angered by his refusal to condemn.

He looked at her, in his eyes a mixture of compassion and understanding. 'My dear, because if they do this thing there'll be jobs for the young people, work for all of those who want it. And with the money they make from that they'll be able to develop the rest of their land.'

He pointed out of the window to the hills that sheltered them, the boundary sharply defined. On one side pine trees, sombre and profitable, on the other the gold and white commingled of gorse and manuka, beautiful and a scourge. 'Look over there, Kirsty. Rangitatau will be beautiful whatever happens. The station is profitable because we've had clear title to our land and access to all of the resources of modern industry to make it so. Why blame the Corporation for using those resources too? In ten years' time their land will be as productive as ours, and in the economic climate of today anything that brings jobs and money into the district must be welcome.'

Elaine's appearance brought him to a halt. Clearly she had washed the signs of grief and shock away, and the look that she bent on Christabel had something of the admonitory to it.

'Like all men, you use logic and think us too emotional when we see things with our hearts,' she said, moving across to link her arm with her husband's. 'But you hate the thought, too, don't you?'

Donald looked sideways at her before nodding, his normally self-contained expression miserable.

It was an intimate moment, one at which Christabel felt like an intruder. And it was broken by the sound of an engine and the baby's cry together.

'Who—*oh*, it's Alex!' said Elaine, peering through the window, on her way to the door. 'I'll see to Stephanie first. Kirsty, you do the necessary, will you.' Her look was arch, conspiratorial; she felt she knew why they were seeing such a lot of Alex Thomassin, and being the darling that she was, it never occurred to her that what he wanted from her stepdaughter was not the wedded bliss she thought the ultimate aim of every woman but something much more basic and primitive.

Struck by her sudden stillness, Donald looked a moment at the downbent head of his daughter before saying heavily, 'I'll go out.'

When they came into the morning room Christabel hadn't moved. A dreadful inertia kept her immobile, but at the sound of Alex's hard tones she lifted her head, averting her eyes from the letter.

'—I'm sorry,' he was saying, the formidable lines of his face set in an expression of complete detachment, those calculating eyes providing the only sign of animation. 'When I saw Mr Panapa this morning he told me about the letter and that he'd posted it yesterday. I flew straight up, hoping that I'd get here before it did.'

Bewildered, afraid as she had never been before, Christabel shook her head. 'What on earth are you talking about?' she asked faintly.

The dark eyes lanced across her face. 'Just explaining that the tribal Corporation and Thomassin Holdings are joint partners in the development.'

He watched as her hand groped to find the back of a chair and gripped it. When she said nothing he resumed in a noncommittal voice, 'I saw the potential of this place three years ago, but it's taken this long to hammer out the details. Unfortunately it was necessary to keep it all secret.'

'Then you—is *that* why . . .?'

Her voice could not frame the words. It hurt to breathe, hurt to even think. The hand that held so tightly to the chair was rigid, the slender fingers bloodless. With the other she touched her mouth before letting it drop again in her side. In her heart was an arid, aching wasteland.

'I'd hoped to tell you myself.' Alex was ignoring her to speak directly to her father. 'I know . . .'

Unable to bear the cool, unemotional voice she burst out brokenly, 'You *know*! What can you know? How to sneak and lie——!'

'*Kirsty!*' Donald's shocked voice broke into her bitter denunciation, startling her into a silence broken only by the deep sobbing breaths she drew.

She could not bear the sight of him, standing so tall, dominating even her father's quiet strength with his dark vitality. Traitor—*betrayer*! For a moment she thought she had screamed the words at him, but even as she put a trembling hand to her mouth she realised her mistake and turned away, eyes brilliant with unshed tears.

'I appreciate your attitude,' Donald said to Alex after a tense moment. His worried eyes sought his daughter's averted profile. 'I'd have preferred it if you'd told us right at the start, but your reasons for not doing that are more than adequate. And I have no intention of making legal objections to your plans.'

For once Alex was at a disadvantage. Through the buzzing in her ears Christabel heard him say with taut composure:

'You make me feel like a heel. I'd have told you if I could, but I believed that I was honour bound to keep silent. I didn't enjoy the situation. I wish I'd been able to get here before that.' His lean forefinger flicked the letter.

Donald shrugged. 'What's done is done. Now, can I offer you a drink? Tea—coffee? Or something stronger?'

'Tea will be fine.'

'Kirsty?' When she didn't move Donald said sternly, 'Kirsty, will you make us tea, please?'

Her head moved in silent acquiescence. 'Yes, of course,' she said with distant politeness, and left them.

Stupid—*stupid* to lose her temper so childishly! It had been years since she had exploded like that. But the turmoil of emotions within her had made it impossible for her to keep cool. Only now when she was alone in the quiet kitchen would she admit that the cause of her fury had been her sudden realisation that Alex's interest had been the development of Rangitatau. She had grown to like him immensely, they all had, and he had fooled them all, making a place for himself in their lives while all the time he had intended nothing but betrayal.

CHAPTER EIGHT

WHILE the kettle hummed and sang Christabel stood with her eyes fixed on the view through the window, imagining the beaches thronged with noisy curious holidaymakers and gaudy sun umbrellas, the water of the bay marred by the buzzing of runabouts and speedboats. The hills she had loved for a lifetime would soon be hidden by high-rise hotels, the warm clear air tainted with the exhaust of vehicles.

Every time she wanted to go out she would have to pass through the hotel grounds. Well, she thought, bitterness twisting her lips, the guests would have to get accustomed to stock trucks and fertiliser loaders trundling through their manicured playground!

The hissing sounds as the kettle boiled over on to the bench brought her back to her surroundings. For a moment her teeth clenched on her bottom lip, so hard that they marked the fine skin, reddening it. Then she switched off at the wall and muttered something her father would not have liked to hear, taking a vicious satisfaction in the obscenity. The memory of Elaine's tear-stained face whipped up a savage anger that overrode her despair and humiliation. It glittered in the stormy green depths of her eyes, tightening the skin over the fragile bones of her face as she opened cake tins and took out afghans and neenish tarts, a solid fruit cake which Donald called instant energy, and covered crackers with cheese and tomato slices.

Elaine was back when she carried the tray through. The atmosphere was a little stiff, but Donald's calm good sense eased matters, and Alex's charm was a great smoothing agent, as no doubt it had been hundreds of times before in similar situations. Silently hating him,

Christabel drank a little tea and wondered when he had first come to realise that in that charm he had a thoroughly unfair weapon. One in a formidable armoury.

From beneath her lashes she watched him, as completely at home in this untidy, comfortable room as he had been in Sarah's parents' enormous, fashionably decorated house. Put him down naked in a pigmy encampment, she thought with smouldering acidity, and within a day he would be at one with his environment, as much a leader as he was here. What was it that made him so totally in command?

A bone-deep confidence, complete sureness. He knew himself. And oh, how cynically he knew other people! That unerring knack for assessing the weaknesses of others gave him self-assurance and made him a dangerous opponent.

Christabel did not know that she had arrived at the same conclusions as some of his dearest business rivals and most devoted associates. To her he was a threat far greater than Greg had ever been.

Something Elaine said made him laugh, the strong white teeth gleaming for a moment as his arrogantly held head was lifted, dark hair gleaming with its red highlights in the rays of the sun.

The slender fingers which held the handle of Christabel's cup trembled as she forced her blind gaze downwards. For a moment everything stilled. In that instant of time while he laughed her body had remembered what it was like to be possessed by him. Every muscle clenched in an agony of need as if some dark fountain of fire pushed through unsuspecting soil to the surface, bringing catastrophe and destruction with it.

Thank God he would not be coming here again. Now that he had accomplished his aim, and it could only have been to charm Donald into accepting the development, he would go his way and never bother them again. And she must convince him that there was nothing here for him, or sooner or later that fiery tide would overwhelm her and she would become his plaything until he tired of her. Oh, it would be rapture while it lasted, fire and passion and excitement, but she knew how bitter the aftertaste would be in her mouth!

His hand, the only part of him in her angle of vision, moved, the long, strong fingers sketched a slight gesture and Elaine laughed again.

'Was that Scott?' Christabel's voice startled even her, it was so constricted. 'No, you stay, Elaine. I'll get him up.'

As a ploy to get out of the room it couldn't have been more transparent, but it worked, and on the way down to Scott's little bedroom Christabel managed to regain some sort of control. Once more feverish memories would have to be buried deep down beneath the conscious levels of her mind, or she would be undone by a craving which was growing each day that passed, feeding on memories imprinted on the cells of her brain and body.

Scott was flushed and inclined to be grumpy, but after a little cuddle and a drink of water his normally sunny temperament reasserted itself.

'Let's go and have some biscuits,' he told her ingenuously, pulling her towards the kitchen. 'I'm hungry, Kirsty.'

'But you're always hungry, darling.'

'It's my tummy,' he confided, his upward glance mischievous.

'Do you think your tummy would be satisfied with a piece of apple?'

He pretended to consider this, then nodded. 'With the skin on.'

'Well, of course!'

She was in the kitchen cutting the big green Granny Smith into quarters when Elaine arrived.

'I'll do that,' she said, hastily putting the tray on to

the bench. 'Kirsty, bring out the milk, will you? I've left it on the table.'

'Where have the men gone?'

Elaine took the knife from her. 'Your father was talking about shifting the flock of ewes.'

Which meant that she had lingered long enough for Alex to have gone. Thank God! If she never saw him again it would be too soon, she thought viciously. In the common idiom, she'd had a gutfull. Her sojourn in the world of the sophisticated people should have prepared her for a man who used sex as a part of his business armoury, but she was still too naïve to be able to cope. And to think she had wondered if she was falling in love with him!

She was smiling bitterly when she came through the door of the morning room, a smile that vanished immediately, for Elaine had been evasive, no doubt on instructions. With a blundering movement she turned, but he caught her wrists and pulled her towards him, the strength of his fingers cruel against the fine bones.

'I want to talk to you.'

She stared stubbornly at his hands, remembering her mother's invariable reaction to a demand as unsubtle as this. 'Want must be your master', Brenda would have said as she had said hundreds of times to Christabel.

'There's nothing to say.' Her voice was cool, but the emotion she hid made her heart beat frantically against his fingers.

'You don't really believe that.' Alex slid his hands to her elbows, pulling her closer as he spoke almost caressingly into her hair. 'I know you're heartbroken about the development of the place, but after the initial period, which will be noisy and dusty and excessively trying, you won't find much difference here.'

She lifted eyes which were a pure flaming green to his, saw the coaxing, half-amused expression with which he was regarding her and knew sheer, naked hatred.

Although her lashes immediately veiled it he saw. His

face hardened, as did his voice. 'All right, so you think me all sorts of a bastard, and you're entitled to. But while you're hating me remember this. The decision to go ahead with the development was made before we met again.'

'Easy enough to say,' she said scornfully, and then, as his words registered, 'What do you mean—*again*?' And could have killed herself for betraying herself so easily.

He laughed softly, his breath warm across her forehead as he pulled her inexorably into his arms. 'Oh, come on, just how stupid do you think I am? I've known for some weeks now that the expensive, worldly Christabel Evans I met in Surfers and the staid Kirsty Grieves of Rangitatau were one and the same.' He paused, but she stood rigid, trying to cope with this new revelation, hearing the words beat around in a brain which suddenly seemed empty of anything else.

Then he said, and he was smiling as he spoke, she could hear it in his voice, 'The very come-hitherish Christabel and the excessively stand-offish Kirsty. Any chance of a split personality, or are you a chameleon?'

'No.' That was all that she could say, and even then her voice felt as though it was coming over hot coals.

'We can't talk here,' he said in sudden impatience, turning her so that they were walking towards the French window. 'We'll head off along the beach.'

Obediently, like a child, Christabel allowed him to urge her through the door and out into the sunlight which lay in mellow serenity across the lawn. With a kind of fatalism she knew that they must get this over and done with and then Alex would go and never come back, and she could get on with the business of living, free from the complications this hideous coincidence had caused in her life.

Neither spoke as they made their way down the path beneath the pohutukawas, but at the base of the bank Alex said calmly, 'Did you really think you could get away with it, Christabel?'

And when she didn't answer he chuckled and took her slender, deceptively fragile hand in his, and they walked the full length of the beach to the little *pa* that divided them from the next bay. He took the narrow sheep track that led to a small plateau where those ancient Maoris had stored their sweet potatoes, as evidenced by the remains of kumara pits in the ground. The grass was longer here, and wiry, tough as the pohutukawa trees which fringed the area. Quite gently Alex pushed her on to the ground and sat down beside her, smiling into her pale face with irony and that unbreakable self-assurance which had the effect of suddenly stiffening her sinews.

He found the situation amusing and he was totally confident of her, she could see that confidence in the hard, handsome lines of his face and the cool survey of his eyes.

'What shall we discuss first, Rangitatau or your metamorphosis?'

She looped her fingers around her raised knee, staring out across the blue-green waters of the bay through the Gates to the deeper blue of the sea beyond. 'Rangitatau,' her voice told him, calm, precise, almost placid in its total lack of expression.

'So. We've been working on plans for Rangitatau for three years. They're complete now.' The powerful shoulders lifted in a shrug. 'All that we have to face are the objections. As your father's not going to object that leaves only the conservationists. I hope to be able to prove that as we envisage the development, the environment will be enhanced, not destroyed.'

'I see.' She could have asked him what could enhance the exquisite picture before her, but she knew that it would be no use. To him Rangitatau was no more than a means to make profits.

A note of irritation, instantly suppressed, roughened his voice. 'All right, I know that nothing is going to recompense you for loss of privacy—but at least give me credit for some aesthetic appreciation!'

Like his appreciation of beautiful women? 'Oh, I do,' she said, and before he could take her up on that charged statement, 'What about the County Council?'

'They're delighted,' he told her with dry emphasis. 'They get eleven miles of sealed road, a hefty increase in rates to spend in the rest of their area, and a thriving new asset. Jobs, Christabel, for people such as you who would otherwise have to leave home.'

She did not tell him of her plans to go to university. What would be the use? He saw her as a lightweight, easily persuaded into almost anything. And, she thought, squirming with bitter humiliation, he had every reason to feel like that after the way she had behaved on that first meeting.

'Congratulations,' she said smoothly. 'I suppose you were up here for talks with them when you—just arrived—on our doorstep?'

'Correct.' He leaned back against the grassy bank, hands clasped behind his head, his face shuttered, a handsome stranger with such cold purpose in his expression that she was repelled by it. But she was repelled by everything she knew of him.

'Then why did you allow Dad to persuade you to stay?'

He didn't react to the scorn in her tones. 'Because I fancied you.'

'You—you *fancied* me?'

His lashes lifted to reveal opaque dark eyes which rested with meaning on her mouth and the high swell of her breasts and the slender length of her legs. 'Just that,' he drawled insolently. 'I was due for a holiday and you intrigued me, a pretty mixture of sophistication and naïvety. I decided it would be enjoyable to find out which you were. And it was, very enjoyable. You fascinated me. Now I realise that it was because my subconscious had made the connection. But at the time I kept getting tantalising little glimpses of another Kirsty, of several other Kirstys.' His voice deepened.

'One was silk-clad and very upmarket, but the other—
ah, the other Kirsty was the one who haunted my
dreams. She was warm and excited and she lay against
me moaning——!'

Christabel leaped up, only to find her feet taken away
from beneath her in a tackle which would have brought
down a rugby forward. She landed heavily, the breath
knocked out of her. Gasping, she fought for several
moments to regain it. When she could turn her
attention to other things it was to find Alex holding her
beneath him, his expression implacable.

'And *that* Kirsty,' he said through lips that barely
moved as his head came down, 'that Kirsty is the one I
want to see again, warm and willing and as
incandescent as a sky full of fireworks, beautiful to see
and touch and feel . . .'

His voice died as his mouth met hers in a kiss that
hurt her, pressing the inner surface of her lip against the
barrier of her teeth until she whimpered and opened
them so that he was able to explore deeply the soft
recesses of her mouth.

Sensation divorced from emotion, pure as a sharp
sword of pain swept through her body. Every nerve
contracted, then relaxed into an aching anticipation as
his mouth roved down the arched line of her throat,
making her wait for the touch of it, every movement
revealing experience allied to a very great natural talent
for lovemaking.

Christabel sighed voluptuously, relishing the heat
which rose from deep inside her. It was familiar yet
strange. In Alex's dim bedroom she had been so
bemused that much of what had happened had passed
her by. But although she had forgotten the swift curling
sensations caused by his mouth on her skin she
recognised them now and greeted them as old friends,
her body taut with a hungry desire.

Somehow his shirt had been pulled free at the waist.
Now her hands found their way between the cotton and

his skin, stroking up the long line of his backbone, her fingertips incredibly sensitised so that she could feel the rippling strength of his muscles beneath the fine skin, the faint dampness impeding her movements so very slightly.

Beneath her bare skin the grass prickled. She moved a shoulder blade experimentally and he whispered, 'Undo my shirt.'

She fumbled, and he laughed and helped her to spread the shirt out, and while he was about it slid her pretty sunfrock over her head, then he pulled her down on to the shirt and said in thick, husky voice, 'My God, you're beautiful! Perfect as a Greek statue.'

'So are you,' she whispered, pressing feverish little kisses to his warm brown shoulder, smooth as oiled silk in the sunlight.

She felt his tension, knew a like tension in herself and her teeth nipped into the mound of a muscle. He swore and then laughed, his dark face reckless in the sunlight as he bent his head to her breast. His tongue traced a path across the smooth white skin to reach its destination. Beneath the lips which fastened ravenously on to it the nub hardened. Heat suffused her, a great wave of it. She would despise herself for this in an hour's time, yet there was no way she could resist him. Something, some part of her beyond control beyond reason, craved this sensual gratification like a drug. Nothing else mattered, not even her honour or her pride, compared to the sensations Alex was making her feel and the knowledge that he felt something of the same thralldom as she did. Perhaps any beautiful woman could wring this kind of reaction from him, but she doubted it. He, too, was possessed of a need for this savage oblivion so great that nothing took precedence.

His hands slid to her rib cage, fastened tightly around the narrow waist and he lifted her, sliding down the tiny bikini briefs which had been the remaining barrier between them. Sunlight dazzled her eyes; she closed them and stroked his shoulders while he dispatched the rest of his clothes with a few swift movements.

Then he was back with her and she smiled as she welcomed him, arms twined tightly around his back, her hips moving in slow provocation beneath him.

'How long?' he asked her, and when she opened her eyes, clearly bewildered, 'When was the last time you had a lover?'

She shook her head, angry with him for intruding with words into this turbulent realm of senses.

'How *long*?' he persisted, but she covered his mouth with her own. He groaned but that immense self-control held and he whispered, 'Tell me, Christabel.'

'Ages.' There was a reason why she should not let him know that she had never had another lover: she didn't know why, but she knew that he mustn't know. 'Please, Alex, don't torment me . . .'

Her voice trailed away as he smiled, dark face clenched with the passion her writhing body and warm lips aroused. 'Not the handsome vet?'

'No.'

'Never?'

'Oh, God, no. Never!' Was that her voice, shivering dazed with desire?

'Good.' And at last he responded to her demands in a sensual storm of such magnitude that when it was over she lay breathless and quiescent in his arms, her breasts rising and falling against the hard wall of his chest as she tried for breath.

'How do you do it?' he groaned, his mouth making tiny kisses against the pale gold of her throat. 'God, you make me forget everything in the desire to have you, and then I can't get enough of your delectable body. Witch, beautiful, inviting, tantalising witch, with your sea-green eyes and your skin like warm satin and your body that calls to mine with a siren's song . . .' He laughed deep in his throat as she trembled, aroused once more by the deep sensuous notes of his voice.

'You're insatiable,' he whispered, his fingers cupping the high young breast, then moving in a slow deliberate slide to her hip and across the tight plane of her stomach before exploring even further. 'And you make me insatiable too, witch. What do you want me to do now?'

Oh God, all that she wanted was the erotic oblivion of his body. Drowsy, slumbrous eyes met his and saw in the dark depths passion and triumph and mastery. He welcomed this physical servitude she experienced, for it relegated her to the status of one of his women, reinforcing his arrogant dominance.

I hate you, she thought, I despise you and myself, but in spite of herself her breath began to quicken and she lifted a boneless hand to run it languidly over his hips, fascinated by the way the muscles tightened beneath so light a touch.

'You're a silent lover,' he said. 'Shall I make you speak?'

Angered, she lifted her gaze to his, then closed her eyes, because he was laughing at her, the glitter of passion beneath the heavy lids mixed with the sardonic mockery she hated.

Perhaps he took that silent refusal as a challenge, for his mouth swooped to tease the soft globes of her breasts, but when he was satisfied that her hunger was as great as his he refused her the release her frantic body demanded, withholding himself until she whispered, 'Please, Alex, please! Don't stop, not now, not now,' not even aware of the abject surrender in her words. Then he smiled with satisfaction and the torment ceased in the powerful intrusion of his body into hers.

This time it was slower, more restrained, yet the sensations were even more exquisite. It was as though he was determined to drown her in the glory, prove to her that this was what she had been made for, this incredible explosion of sensation, mind and heart overwhelmed so that all that she was conscious of were her needs, his needs and the sating of them.

Afterwards, of course, came the shame.

'We can't stay here for the rest of the day,' he said on a note of laughter. 'Are you going to get dressed?'

Trembling with reaction, Christabel pulled her clothes on, eyes lowered so that she didn't see him do the same. Her lip quivered; she bit it to stop the betraying little movement and got stiffly to her feet, walking across the tiny plateau to where the path wound down on to the beach. I'll never be able to come here without feeling this acrid taste of abasement, she thought wearily, exhausted by their lovemaking and the bitter knowledge of her degradation.

For Alex this was just a pleasant interlude with a responsive, willing woman. No doubt he would leave and when he thought of her, in between the exigencies of big business, it would be with the cynical knowing thoughts of a man who knew exactly what she was.

She stiffened as he came up behind her. If he said anything . . .

But he said nothing, just took her hand in his and set off down the path to the beach, leading so that if she tripped his lean body would take the impact. Impersonally protective, she thought, and hated him for it, hated him for proving that she was so easily seduced, like all the other stupid women who had found rapture in his bed.

Humiliation of a strength she had never experienced before ached through her body. Wanting nothing more than to crawl away into a dark corner and lick her wounds she was forced to behave in as reasonable manner as possible because back at the homestead Elaine and Donald would be waiting and she could not bear for them to know of her weakness.

But halfway along the beach Alex drew her up into the sandhills and pulled her down beside him to rest on the thick couch of marram grass which prevented the treacherous sand from advancing.

'I have to go immediately,' he said abruptly. 'I flew up from Auckland and the plane's still at the airstrip. But I'll be back as soon as I can. I'll give you an address——'

Later, she would realise that it would have been better to agree to his plans and carry out her own in secret, but pride, the desire to show him that she had some strength of mind, forced her into speech.

'You needn't bother on my account. I won't be writing.'

There was an ominous silence before his fingers tangled in the hair at the nape of her neck and tipped her face up for inspection. Calm, coldly composed, she met the icy impact of his stare without flinching.

'Indeed?' he said through his teeth. 'What is this?'

'Nothing.' She held his gaze, refusing to allow any bitterness to show. 'It's just that I have no intention of making myself available for any more amorous interludes in your life.'

His glance narrowed, became fierce and stabbing. Behind the handsome face the sharp, brilliant brain processed the information his senses fed him.

Christabel endured the hard assessment until he finally relinquished his grasp of her hair. 'Hating yourself, darling?' the mocking voice enquired silkily.

With stony control she retorted, 'That's none of your business, Alex. Just don't go making any plans that include me, now or ever. I don't want to know.'

He lifted a hand and put it on her thigh, smiling as she tried to knock it off. The strong fingers tightened, impressing themselves into the taut skin, then relaxed as he said coolly, 'You hate yourself for succumbing and so you hate me for taking what you so generously offered. You know, you've got a hang-up about purity, my lovely lady Christabel. No doubt, before you marry, you'll feel impelled to confess all your past love affairs. Your future husband won't like that much.'

'It won't concern you,' she said icily, her throat so strained that the words hurt.

His hand slid up her leg to the narrow lace at the edge of her briefs. He watched her as colour seeped from her skin at the intimate, careless caress.

It was a punishment. This, he was telling her, is the sort of woman you are, open to any man's hands, any man's touch. And the horror of it was that he was wrong, for it was only he who possessed the key to unlock the passionate responses of her body.

As if sickened by her passive acceptance of his touch he jerked his hand away, asking in a hard voice that emphasised the sudden glitter deep in his eyes, 'Won't you be my mistress, Christabel? Oh, I realise that you can't leave Elaine yet, not until she's fully recovered, but I could get across to see you quite often. And when things are settled here you can come across to live with me in Melbourne.' His voice thickened. 'I can be exceedingly generous when I'm pleased—and satisfied. You wouldn't have to model dresses, I'd buy them to decorate your beautiful body. And jewellery, within reason. Not if you're too greedy, of course; no one takes me for a ride.'

Stop it, *stop it*! her mind screamed in a tumult of shame and despair. I can't bear it! But she had to. It was all part of her punishment, to hear him proposition her with such casual crudeness, making it only too clear exactly how he thought of her. Erect, her whole body stiff with rejection, she said nothing as he went on savagely, 'You'll have to curb that devastating enthusiasm, of course. I don't share. But when you no longer excite me I'll be generous, just as generous as you are with your favours. You won't lose by it, I promise.'

'No!' she exclaimed harshly, jumping to her feet.

Alex stayed seated, looking up at her with insulting thoroughness, eyeing her long legs and the soft swell of her breasts, the pulse which beat heavily at the base of her throat, the pale, cold features above it, redeemed from total lack of colour by the ripe redness of a mouth too roughly kissed and eyes that were as stormy as the sea in an easterly.

'No?' A dark brow lifted and he leaned back on an elbow, the opposing leg raised at the knee. Totally relaxed, big and dark against the thin covering of grass. A hunting beast, waiting only for the first false move to leap in for the kill.

'Come here,' he said softly, watching her as she stopped her instinctive retreat. She could feel his intention beating against her. He wanted to prove how weak she was, how firmly caught by his aura of sensual virility.

Well, she would not. Give me just this self-control, God, she prayed, her will strengthening to meet his challenge. If he touched her she would be lost, but he would not touch her. He wanted her drawn to him by the force of that unwilling attraction, to see her kneel beside him, lost and witless and wanting, dishonoured and humbled because she could not resist the clamour that ran through her body at the sight of him.

Her will held. After a few moments she managed to find the strength to say with hard pride. 'I'm not cut out to be a plaything, Alex. Sorry, but that's the way it is.'

'Oh, but you have an enormous talent for sex,' he said insolently. 'If a life without work bores you I wouldn't mind if you kept your hand in modelling. Provided that you're always in my bed when I want you, of course.'

Momentarily, Christabel closed her eyes, repelled by the calculating effrontery of his suggestion. Anger clotted in her throat, but she swallowed it back, welcoming its warmth and ferocity because it banished the icy despair which had her in its grip.

'Sorry,' she said again, because that was all that she could trust herself to say, then turned and walked back down on to the beach.

The sun had almost set and the air was still and cool as she walked down to where the tide had bared hard sand, carefully avoiding the dimpled patches which were the tuatua nurseries. A couple of days ago she had scraped away a thin layer of sand to show Scott the tiny translucent shellfish. Farther out to sea lurked the adult tuatua, plump and delicious and plentiful, the basis for many a meal.

Now she walked carefully, almost in the waves. A pair of oyster-catchers watched her with beady eyes until she came too close for comfort, then flew farther up the beige sand to join a small flock of elegant pied stilts.

At first she kept her head down, noting the scalloped patterns the receding waves had left on the sand. Until she felt the icy prickle between her shoulder blades that told her he watched. Then she flung up her head and straightened her shoulders, walking away from him without a backward look. Past the house, around the shoreline until she reached the tiny cove at the foot of the southern Gate, and there she stayed until the sun had set in a sultry scarlet sky and Alex was gone.

CHAPTER NINE

THE autumn was long and warm and comparatively dry, exquisite days of blue and gold with nights when the stars made a diamond netting across the sky and the moon rose over the edge of the sea like a great copper gong.

Great weather for construction workers. No one had objected to the development; even the most ardent conservationist was placated by the care taken with the plans, so within a very short time of Alex's departure gangs of men began moving in, surveyors and others who ran around in Land Rovers, measuring and sighting and digging small holes about the place.

The peace of Rangitatau became a thing of the past. Many of the men liked to fish and a few even braved the waves, although the water was really too cold now for swimming.

Then, when Christabel was able to feel relief that those maddened minutes spent in Alex's arms were to be without fruit, the heavy brigades moved in. The air was made dusty and shatteringly noisy as huge bulldozers tore the land and enormous carryalls ran around with loads of topsoil, piling it in heaps across the scarred grass to be used later for landscaping.

A village of sorts sprang up, long rows of single men's quarters and a big social hall. Occasionally men knocked on the door requesting permission to shoot rabbits over the station.

Donald refused them all and looked on, impassive, as 'No Trespassing' signs were posted along the boundary.

'Apparently the management ordered them to be put up,' he said over dinner one night.

'Alex?' Elaine looked surprised. 'That was thoughtful of him.'

'Yes.' Her husband's eyes rested a moment on his daughter's averted face. Kirsty had lost the weight she had gained during the past months and was back to model thinness again. All right for photographs, he supposed, but he had liked her better the way she had been over the summer, tanned and eager, filled with vigour.

Now there were shadows in her eyes and something vital in her had been extinguished. She had retreated to a place where no one could reach her and he ached for her but was unable to help.

'Well, I wish he could put up "No whistling" signs,' Elaine said crisply. 'I hate driving through the camp, I get such a barrage of wolf-whistles each time. I know it's goodhumoured, but I find it . . .'

Her voice trailed away. After a moment Christabel supplied a word: 'Threatening,' she murmured, resuming her attempt at the dinner for which she had no appetite.

'Yes.' Elaine nodded. 'That's it exactly.'

Donald frowned. 'They seem a decent enough bunch of men,' he observed.

But the next morning he took the Land Rover with him and set off towards the pine plantation. About three weeks later he told them laconically that the track through the pines was passable out to the road if they wanted to go that way.

'Courtesy of Alex?' Elaine asked a little archly.

'No.' Donald was offhand. 'I've been intending to upgrade it for some time. It's O.K. now, but take care when you go through.'

That made things a little less claustrophobic, especially as the county road was now almost impassable. It was being upgraded to the standard expected by the tourists who would be spending their holidays at Rangitatau. Not for them potholes and corrugations and bridges with no sides. Machinery was working to provide them with a two-lane highway, sealed to the station gates, all corners wide and sweeping, the bridges railed and safe.

Gone, gone for ever was the peace and the freedom, Christabel thought wearily as from the back of one of the station hacks she watched the gang her father had employed set out three rows of young trees backed by a line of giant bamboo roots along the border. He might call it a windbreak and say that he had been intending to put one up for years, but they all knew that it was a barrier to protect them from the hordes.

'Well, that's how I think of them,' she defended herself in all seriousness when Nate teased her about her choice of words. 'Oh, look at it!' Her arm swept the panorama beneath, the green peaceful fields of the station a vivid contrast to the broken moonscape just through the fence.

'Imagine it in five years' time,' Nate soothed.

'All restaurants and tanning-oil!' she flashed back scathingly.

He grinned, wishing it took something other than anger to banish the defeated look she seemed to have acquired recently.

'You're ever so slightly prejudiced against this development, aren't you?'

A sigh parted her lips. 'Ever so slightly, and you don't have to tell me that it's selfishness, I'm well aware of that. You know, Nate, when my mother took me to Australia I cried every night for years, longing to be back here.'

'It became like Paradise for you,' he said with understanding and compassion for the gawky, bewildered child who had been the innocent victim of her parents' ordinary little tragedy. 'No, more like Shangri-la, inaccessible, the much-desired, the impossible.'

'Oh yes, you know! How do you know?'

He shrugged noncommittally. 'Everyone has a Shangri-la in their lives. A place—or a dream—or a person. Now you feel that yours is being desecrated.'

Such perception made her a little uneasy, but when she searched his face for clues to a hidden meaning there was no sign of it, so she had to accept his observation at its surface value.

'Just that,' she agreed drily. 'I came back and let the serpent in. Or in this case, the caterpillar,' gesturing at the enormous yellow earth-moving machinery.

His kind blue eyes laughed at her. 'Nonsense! Oh, I can understand your unhappiness, but it was going to happen whether or not you came back. Thomassin said it's been in the pipeline for three years, so Donald told me.'

Beneath Christabel her horse made a soft blowing sound through its nostrils, then flicked an ear at a fly. After a moment it dropped its head and began to mouth the grass, not hungrily, merely for something to do.

Pushing the sleeves of her scarlet jersey up to her elbows, Christabel said defensively, 'I know, I know.'

Yet in an irrational part of her brain she did feel that she had been the one to bring this destruction to Rangitatau. Ridiculous, of course, but somehow the bitter pain of her relationship with Alex had become bound up with the rape of the bay. And she blamed Alex for both, the deep personal despair as well as the devastation of all that made life here so tranquil and perfect. Completely without logic—but then where Alex was concerned she was not logical.

Sudden colour flamed across the high cheekbones as she remembered with savage clarity just how very far from sensible she was about him and the old, aching longing suffused her body, calling him back to ease it the only way possible. If he came back and kissed her she would follow him again and lie in his arms, totally subjugated by desire. For it must be desire, this hollow need; only she missed him so, his conversation, his intelligence and incisive wit, his laughter and companionship.

For her there were no pathways through this jungle in which she wandered, no smooth, smiling grassy plains, no sky of promise or hope, only the weary, ever-present struggle to fight her way through to some sort of acceptance.

Alex would not come back. With little idea of how construction jobs like this were organised, Christabel was almost certain that the—whatever was he, owner? director?—whatever—rarely had much to do with the actual work on the site.

But until they took down the big signs that proclaimed 'Thomassin Holdings' she could not escape him.

Sighing, she flicked the reins. The hack lifted his head and she touched him gently with her heels. 'We'd better get back,' she said lightly without looking at Nate. 'Or we'll be late for the party.'

'We don't have to go,' he said quietly, aware of something weary in her mood.

'Of course we do. Marguerite and Sam would never forgive us if we didn't appear. Anyway,' trying hard to infuse the right amount of enthusiasm into her voice, 'it will be fun.'

It was, too. Their hosts were amiable and not too bright, but they possessed the gift of laughter and their vivacity was such that much of their conversation passed for wit. Christabel danced and laughed and drank a little more wine than usual, trying to convince herself that she was having fun, and if she felt a million years older than anyone else in the crowded rooms, only she knew of it.

That was what self-contempt did to you. Made you feel old and tired with a bone-deep weariness; made you feel as though you had lost half of yourself and would never find it again, and never cease mourning your loss.

Of course she wasn't going to mourn for ever. Nowadays women didn't die of shame or shut themselves away in convents. They picked themselves up and got on with life and living, firmly banishing the past.

And that was what she would do when this nagging, dull pain that ate up her vigour and vitality was gone.

There was one bad moment during the evening, and even that was not too shattering because she had been tensed for it ever since Penny Mountain's ash-blonde hair glimmered into sight on the edge of her vision.

So when the high, little-girl voice said, with perfect clarity and the merest trace of malice, 'Why, Kirsty, what happened to that ab-so-lute-ly *delicious* man you had with you at the Muirheads' do?' it was easy enough for her to smile.

She was rather proud of that smile. It was slightly tolerant and even conspiratorial as her eyes met Nate's.

'Back in Australia. Sorry, Jenny, but he's a big man.'

Penny gave an affected little shiver, the large doll's eyes very round and sharp. 'I know, you're laughing at me because big men turn me on, but don't they you, Kirsty?' That wide gaze flicked to Nate, standing with his arm loosely around Christabel's waist. 'I mean, Nate isn't *small*,' she pointed out sweetly. 'Oh, look, I've made you blush! Fancy still being able to.'

Christabel lifted her brows. 'I meant "big" as in "important",' she said drily. 'When you have an industrial and commercial empire depending on you you tend to move around a lot.'

'Oh, he struck me as a very fast mover,' Penny agreed with a demure little smile. 'Is there any chance of him coming back? I mean, you and he obviously knew each other well.'

Nate's arm tightened, but Christabel managed a laugh. Let Penny see that one of her barbs had drawn blood and she'd be like a terrier worrying a rat, determined to make a kill.

'Not that well,' she returned pleasantly, allowing her gaze to meet the smaller woman's full on. 'Alex is a law unto himself, but he'll probably be making flying visits across.' She grinned. 'Shall I ring you if he calls in to see us?'

Penny joined in the general laughter at her expense, but couldn't resist saying, 'Oh no, I wouldn't expect that of you, Kirsty. I mean, sisterhood is a wonderful thing, but when it comes to men . . .!'

Well, Christabel wasn't going to deny her her chance to save face. That made honours about even.

But when they were almost home through the thick night Nate said casually, 'Penny seemed rather bitchy about Alex Thomassin. Don't you get on well with her?'

'Oh, you know Penny.'

'Everybody knows Penny, but why should she blame you if the man wasn't attracted?'

'Well, she couldn't blame herself, could she? That's not Penny's way.' She tried hard to banish the faint note of defensiveness from her voice, aware that it was a dead giveaway.

His quiet chuckle reassured her. 'Did you fight at school?'

'Oh, yes. We took one look at each other and that was it.' Leaning her head back against the headrest, she said contemplatively, 'I think why she dislikes me now is because I was such an ugly tyke at school and she was so pretty, yet I ended up being a model. She, like most people, doesn't realise that looks as such are not really necessary.'

The headlights swung on to the two white posts marking the cattlestop; there was the cold rattle of iron bars beneath the car, then Nate turned the lights and the engine off. It was very quiet, the night so dark that the blackness seemed tangible. Clouds had covered the sky and there was no wind. When it did come it would probably be from the north.

'Someone's still up,' Nate remarked. 'Or were they going to leave a light on for you?'

'No, they're up. That's the sitting room. I hope it's not the baby.'

He got out and came around to the door. 'Teething?'
Nate was the oldest of a large family.

'You'd better believe it. Dad says they're getting their
teeth earlier and earlier.'

He laughed. 'Well, I won't come in.' As they stopped
at the door he tipped her chin back and went on softly,
'Whatever you looked like at primary school you are
most certainly beautiful now.'

His kiss was sweet, not tentative, not demanding, and
Christabel responded with guilty appreciation. Stupid
to go through life feeling as though any contact with
another man was a blatant infidelity to Alex, but that
was the way things were and after a moment she broke
the kiss. Tonight, however, Nate refused to accept her
indication of enough and drew her back into his arms,
bending his head to touch his mouth to hers. At first
she stiffened, but through her wariness there came
voices and she recognised them.

When Donald opened the door it was to see his
daughter locked in Nate's arms in an embrace about
which there could be no misconceptions.

As if the sound of the door opening took some
time to penetrate the mists she freed herself slowly
and turned towards them, lips red in a pale face, her
eyes very green and bright as they moved from her
father's startled countenance to that of the man next
to him.

'Hello, Alex,' she said, a slight breathlessness evident
in her voice. 'Back on a flying visit?'

Perhaps she convinced Nate that there was nothing
more than the normal awareness of male and female
between them, but if she did it was without Alex's cooperation. That first swift glance told her that he was
deadly angry with the kind of rage that kills, and
although she was frightened by the molten sheen in the
dark eyes and the cruel jutting line of his jaw she was
stimulated too. If they made love now he would hurt
her, but it would be pain that she would enjoy. . . .

Fiercely clamping down on forbidden desires, she waited while Nate and her father exchanged a few rather trite sentences. Her lashes were lowered but she could see him with her skin, the dark rage swiftly subdued but still there, and she knew he was watching her, his gaze like a brand on her body.

Suddenly she shivered. Immediately Nate said, 'Sorry, I shouldn't be keeping you out in the cold. I'll see you tomorrow, Kirsty.'

'Yes.' They had decided to go on a hike with other members of the Forest and Bird Society along a track through bush and glorious coastal scenery to an old whaling station. She had been looking forward to it in the apathetic way she viewed everything nowadays, but suddenly she didn't want to go. Alex might despise her, but his presence made her feel gloriously, vibrantly alive and she wanted to be where he was.

But she would go, of course.

And go she did, first making sure that she wasn't left alone with Alex. She didn't care if he noticed her elaborate manoeuvres to that end; he could draw what conclusions he liked. For her own self-respect she had to prevent any repetition of what had happened last time.

It was a lovely day, cool enough so that the long walk over some of Northland's steepest coastal hills wasn't too exhausting, yet the sun shone from a sky decorated with great whipped cream clouds. The walk through the bush brought her a certain serenity of mind and the company was pleasant and interesting. Of course, when she was with Nate she always enjoyed herself. He was a darling, rock-strong beneath that quiet exterior, undemanding yet stimulating.

But as they drove bumpily back along the plantation track the bright radiance of the day seemed to dim. Fatalistically Christabel knew that she had only managed to put off the confrontation she so dreaded, not avoided it. And she knew that she would rather fight with Alex than make love with Nate—or any other man.

Sure enough he was waiting for her on the terrace as she came through after a shower, long legs stretched out before him, hands steepled in front.

'Where's Elaine?'

He got to his feet, arrogantly sure of himself. 'She and Scott are picking pipis. I'm baby-sitting.'

'Oh.' She looked sideways, met his implacable stare and said swiftly, 'I'll go down and help them.'

'No,' he said calmly, the brilliant eyes holding hers. 'You'll stay here and listen to me. I've been searching out a few facts and I've learnt quite a bit about you, Christabel, my innocent siren.'

'Don't *call* me that!' White-lipped, she flung away from him, was casually caught by the shoulder and just as casually held against him, his arm an iron bar across her breasts.

Her sudden tremor took them both by surprise. His arm tightened, then relaxed. Very coolly, his breath stirring the tendrils of hair at her temples, he said, 'We can stay like this while we talk or I can let you go. Which?'

Through lips that were dry and stiff she answered, 'You can let me go. I'll listen. Just don't expect me to agree with whatever gossip you've dredged up about me.'

'No gossip.' He waited until she had sat down, her glance obstinately bent towards the floor, before resuming. 'Surprisingly little gossip, in fact. Not even everyone was convinced that you and Greg Bardsley were lovers, in spite of the fact that he has been at some pains to give that impression.'

Goaded, she flashed him a bitter glance her expression so controlled that she looked like the porcelain doll Elaine kept on a corner of the sofa.

'I've stopped that,' he said. 'He'll keep his filthy tongue still from now on.'

'Oh, you are so *kind*!'

He laughed without humour. 'You don't hate *him*, do you, and yet he was the one who betrayed you. I made no pretence of loving you.'

'No, but you knew that I was—that I wasn't myself.'

'You were drunk,' he agreed, apparently not noticing her flinch. 'Only it wasn't the champagne, was it, Christabel? It was a heady brew of revenge and desire and bitterness, aimed directly at Bardsley. You wanted him to suffer the torments of the damned and so you made sure that the poor bastard got what you thought he deserved. It was because he was berserk that night at the visions he had of you in my bed that he betrayed himself to Fliss.'

'I suppose I knew that you'd blame me for the fact that they broke up,' she said in trembling tones. 'Who fed you this—this concoction of innuendoes and half-truths? Or did you come up with such a disgusting scenario yourself? It sounds like you.'

'So you admit there is some truth to it?'

'Yes, I was drunk,' she said baldly, the words crashing around in her head. 'That's the whole truth.'

'For some reason you'd like me to believe that.' His voice was harsh but that immense self-control still held. 'Why? You were slightly affected by alcohol, but that was as far as it went. I watched your intake. You knew what you were doing.'

Christabel had been staring at her knees, her hands clenched tightly together in her lap. Now she relaxed them, counting slowly to herself.

'I was drunk,' she said, finding a perverse pleasure in the repetition of the word. 'I suppose it's more satisfying to your ego if you believe I was sober.'

'Did you love your mother, Christabel?'

The total change of subject jolted her. 'What?'

He shrugged, watching her closely. 'What was your mother like? She hated life here, but she stuck it out for years, so I presume she had determination. I know she pushed you into being a model and that she worked herself. Presumably she had scruples about being supported by Donald, so she had integrity. She certainly had an old-fashioned code of morals because you're still unable to overcome that earlier conditioning, aren't you? Although you thought you were in love with him you kept Bardsley dangling until he was desperate, you hate me because I can make you——'

Blood rushed to her head. So swiftly that she didn't even realise she was moving she jumped to her feet, hands pressed to her ears to shut out the cool judgment in his voice.

'*No!*' she whirled and was caught again. Strong fingers dragged her hands from their place and he looked down into her white face with hard insistence.

'Yes.' He was merciless. 'You know it, Christabel, but for some reason you refuse to face it. We're not going to get anywhere without honesty. Why do you refuse to admit that when I touch you you forget everything your mother taught you, every precept and principle and shibboleth that's buried deeply in your subconscious? Why? Is it because you're trying for the kind of emotional self-sufficiency that your mother was so proud of?'

She would never forgive him for this. *Never!* Such probing belonged to a psychologist's couch, to a situation where trust reigned.

'What are you trying to do?' she asked exhaustedly. 'Destroy me? Emotion has nothing to do with the way I—with *us!*'

A muscle flicked by the hard beautiful mouth, the only sign of humanity in the carved mask of his features. 'That's what you want so fervently to believe, but you know, just as I know, that it's not true. Sex is only a part of what we could have if you'd only open up to it instead of convincing yourself that you're no better than a whore.'

'That's how I feel,' she said with cruel directness. 'That's how you make me feel.'

She winced at the pain as his hands clenched on her wrists. Then she was free, flung from him as though she contaminated him to land breathless and trembling in a heap on the cushions of the cane sofa.

'Very well then,' he said, icily composed. 'If that's the way you feel that's the way I'll treat you. How much do you think your favours are worth, my lovely lady Christabel? Not as much as an experienced courtesan, of course, but I feel sure that losing your virginity must command an extra bonus. As must the swift, wholehearted response——'

'Stop it,' she whispered, so close to tears that she could barely speak through the tightness in her throat. 'Please, just leave me alone.'

'Why? That's one thing about a whore—she's always available.'

A cruel hand forced her chin upwards. One look into the mask of lust that was his face and she shuddered, afraid as she had never been in her life before. Beneath his Australian tan he was pale with an anger so great that only his eyes showed colour and they were almost black, glittering with fury beneath the straight satyr's brows.

She remembered wondering once about the dark red tints in his hair. Now she knew that that formidable self-control hid a temper of terrifying violence.

'Yes,' he said, his fingers sliding around the line of her jaw in a caress which was sensuous and threatening. 'So now, my beautiful, let's talk terms, shall we?'

Christabel closed her eyes, fighting desperately for calm. Her stupidity had brought her to this pass, stupidity and the desire to hurt, and she was reaping the whirlwind. She did not need to think through her situation, intuition warned her that he was very close to real violence and that he would enjoy whatever torment he devised for her. She could hear his breathing deliberate, steady, feel the dormant strength in the lean fingers that cupped her chin, and in spite of her danger, in spite of the humiliation, knew a sudden burgeoning of desire deep within her. Her breath caught in a throat aching with tension.

'We discussed this once before,' she said huskily. 'I still feel the same way, Alex.'

If he noticed the thin note of pleading buried deep in her tones he gave no indication.

He bent his head, taking his time about it so that his image filled her vision and then blurred. So sensitive was her skin to him that she could feel the approach of his mouth. Unconsciously her lips parted and lashes drooped over her widened eyes. When the kiss came her mouth clung to his, but he merely touched lips, then pulled away, straightening up to walk across the terrace.

'No,' he said, the deep voice cold and unemotional. 'We both know that the only place that will get us is bed. And keen though I am to sate myself in your delectable body I think we should get things straightened out first.'

Christabel winced. Betrayed once more by her body, she ached with frustration, watching him hungrily as he stood with his back to her, staring out across the bay. A wind sang a forlorn song around the eaves, lifting into a whining crescendo that rattled the sash.

So lost in each other they had not even noticed that the sun was gone, hidden by a rolling mass of grey clouds.

Beneath Alex's shirt the muscles moved easily as he pushed the window to, clicking it into place. Oh God, she thought wearily, I must be totally depraved to feel like this about a man I despise!

Some movement through the pohutukawas caught his eye and he leaned forward, broad shoulders and the proud head silhouetted against the light. Christabel's mouth dried. She touched her tongue to her lips, racked with desire.

Before she could hide it he turned, the cold eyes resting on her face, delicately flushed, eyes and mouth hungry yet submissive.

'Elaine's back,' he said, and smiled as the hot colour broke through her skin.

CHAPTER TEN

AFTER that Alex treated her with a kind of aloof courtesy which had her by turns furiously, savagely angry and yearningly desirous. He spent a lot of time at the site, even more in conference with the County Council; flew to Wellington to discuss things with the government and on the way back spent a day and a night in Auckland where, so he told Donald and Elaine, he left his private secretary with enough work to keep him occupied while he spent the weekend at Rangitatau.

'And then I'll have to go,' he told them over breakfast on Saturday morning. 'Much as I enjoy staying here, I have other commitments.'

The brilliant gaze lingered a moment on Christabel's downbent face, but when she looked up it had moved to laugh at Scott, crossly vociferous that his idol should be deserting him.

'Come back,' he demanded. 'For a holiday, Alex, please? I'll take you out in mine boat, then.'

Not only Scott listened with indrawn breath for the answer. Christabel was furious with herself, but she had to know if he was planning to return.

'Some time, I promise,' he said noncommittally, and with that they had to be content.

During these few days she had been forced to admit that she craved for him like an addict deprived of his fix. Whenever he was there she felt vividly, vitally alive, even though it was obvious to her, if to nobody else, that since that last cataclysmic quarrel he had been avoiding her.

Perhaps he no longer wanted her, or more probably, he felt she would be too much trouble. After all, why should he bother with a resentful mistress when no doubt he could snap his fingers and acquire one who was more than willing?

Reluctantly, because it added to her sense of shame, she admitted to herself that if he kissed her and then asked her to go with him she would leave Rangitatau without a backward glance. The physical attraction between them was so strong that it was only when they quarrelled, or were apart, that she could think.

That day was overcast, a good day for fishing, Donald decided. So he and Alex went out to do the necessary chores around the station before taking off in the launch with an ecstatic Scott to a special position 'handed down only to the oldest Grieves' son' Donald explained teasingly, where enormous, delicious hapuka lurked.

'And I'll cook them for you for dinner,' Elaine promised, waving them goodbye. 'Now, how do you feel about gardening, Kirsty? It's going to rain soon and I'd like to get fertiliser on before it happens. Which means removing the odd weed.'

Well, anything was better than brooding and wishing she didn't have to go to the Stevensons' party tonight with Nate. More than anything she wanted to stay close to home with Alex, feasting her eyes on him when he wasn't watching, feeding that hunger which sharpened the prominent bones of her face and gave her eyes a lonely, feverish quality.

Of course she would go, and she would make sure that Nate hadn't taken that fervent embrace last weekend too seriously, and when she came home after midnight she wouldn't do what her body urged and slip through the door into her great-grandmother's bedroom and slide naked under the sheet to join Alex.

Because he would take her, enjoy what desperation made her offer and then humiliate her with his arrogant carelessness. If she could only fix in her mind the fact that when he looked at her he saw a mistress, a woman to possess, not a human being with needs and desires and validity!

And why this should be so important was one thing she refused to probe into, because she was afraid. After all, that was how she saw him, surely? As a magnificent male specimen who somehow forced from her body the most exquisite, ravishing sensations.

Oh, she admired his brain, enjoyed his conversation, found him a stimulating and amusing companion, one who shared most of her interests and could discuss them with a hard, incisive judgment, but that was not important.

Her gloved hand forced the fork into the ground, jerked it viciously and withdrew while she seized the weed and yanked it free. Although the cloud cover was low it was warm enough to raise a sweat, and she rubbed her forehead with her arm, leaving a smear of dirt across the fine skin. Just along the border Elaine was humming softly as she worked, the pile of weeds in the barrow growing rather more quickly than she had hoped. Stephanie slept quietly in the pram.

Christabel caught her lower lip between her teeth and bit, hard. Of course she was not interested in Alex, except for his physical attributes. Why, if she admitted any further interests that would come perilously close to respect, and perhaps regard. Even then her mind shied away from the word which hovered on the periphery of her mind.

One simply didn't fall in love with men who treated one like he had treatd her. Did one?

No, not love. Lust. It must be, and when he left it would fade, as all appetites faded. It *must*.

After lunch she wrote letters, helped Elaine prepare part of the dinner and watched a little television. Anything to take her mind off the man who was becoming an obsession.

The men arrived back, triumphant and slightly sunburnt, bearing three large, ugly fish, one of which was Scott's. No, he hadn't actually caught it, because hapuka lived so far down that they were too heavy for him to pull up, but he had helped Daddy catch it.

Elaine laughed and kissed him, sent him off for a bath and asked Christabel if she would supervise.

'Of course; come on, my big brave fisherman, and you can tell me about the one that got away,' she teased, and of course he said indignantly,

'But none did, Kirsty. We catched them all.'

From behind came Alex's voice, cool and with a note of malice. 'Never mind, Scottie, it happens to everyone sooner or later.'

Christabel froze. There had been a very definite edge to the comment. Even Scott noticed it, for he sent a puzzled look upwards.

'Not us, today. Not *you*, Alex.'

'Touching faith of one too young to realise that nobody can win them all all the time,' said Alex. His voice changed. 'Yes, me too, Scott. Even your beloved Kirsty.'

And he smiled and swung on past them down to his bedroom door, tall and dominating in jeans and a thin shirt.

So that was it. He had made it quite obvious. He had decided not to bother with his pursuit any longer.

While she bathed Scott's squirming little body and drank white wine before dinner and ate food that tasted like cardboard in her mouth the knowledge beat in her brain, almost deafening her.

Pain shafted through her, making each breath she drew like a knife in her chest. Yet pride lifted her head and brought vivacity to her speech so that to anyone else she seemed to sparkle.

Alex lifted his glass to his hostess. 'A delicious meal, thank you. You must be one of the world's great cooks. And beautiful with it.'

Elaine smiled at the compliment, her expression filled with gaiety and humour. 'You're a flatterer, Alex, but I don't mind. It's easy to look good when you feel well. And when your stepdaughter watches you like a hawk for any sign of tiredness.' She smiled fondly across the table. 'When Kirsty arrived here I was in a sad state, believe me. Between her and Donald I've been cosseted and loved back into good health.'

'So you're ready to get back into the saddle again?' Alex sounded no more than conversationally interested, a friend asking.

'Yes. Yesterday I had a clearance from the doctor.'

Alex smiled at her, all of his immense charm evident. 'I'm so glad.' Then his glance switched to Christabel and he asked softly, 'And what will you be doing, Christabel, when you leave here?'

'Go to university,' she told him baldly. 'I'm going to do law.'

And knew a savage satisfaction at the flash of astonishment in the dark eyes. It was gone in a second, of course, but just this once she had astounded him.

'Good for you,' he said. 'That should keep you busy for a few years to come.'

Perhaps she was being over-sensitive, but she could almost hear the corollary. 'And out of my hair'.

Well, she would be only too pleased never to see him again. She lifted eyes that were cool and clear and limpid, met his enigmatic smile with one of her own.

'Very busy,' she agreed. 'It's a long-held ambition.'

'No ambitions to marry?' The long fingers turned the blown wine-glass with the same sure gentleness with which they caressed a woman's skin.

Christabel swallowed, for a moment gripped by a storm of emotion compounded of desire and hatred and pain. In a slightly lower voice than normal she said, 'No, none at all. I've not met the right man yet, you see.'

She was devoutly thankful for the telephone's shrill summons. Not so thankful, though, when Alex said something about a call he was expecting and followed her into the hall.

'Kirsty, I'm so sorry, but I'll have to give tonight's party a miss.' Nate sounded slightly harassed but not brokenhearted. 'Poor old John's got a viral 'flu and Mary Harrison's bitch, the one she imported from Australia, is whelping. Making rather heavy weather of it, unfortunately. You know Mary, she's as good as a vet herself and not one to panic, but she wants me there.'

Christabel looked up, met the cold contempt in Alex's eyes without flinching. 'Of course you must help,' she agreed, her voice warm and sympathetic. 'Don't give it another thought. To tell the truth, I'm not very keen on going myself.'

There was a relieved note in his voice. 'You're a darling! 'Bye, now.'

'A darling?' Alex watched as she replaced the receiver, 'I could think of many things to call you, but a darling is not one of them. A tease, a flirt, a coquette—oh, there are plenty of names for women like you. Are you going to enjoy breaking that poor fool's heart?'

'Don't be so melodramatic,' she snapped, so angered by his taunting, unsparing assessment that she conveniently forgot her own fears for Nate. 'Hearts don't break, Alex, as I'm sure you're well aware.'

Her attempt to leave his suffocating presence was foiled by his hands at her elbows pulling her so close that she could feel his breath across her forehead, hear the muted thunder of the heart that beat against her splayed hands. He had his own scent and to her it was an aphrodisiac more potent than any love-philtre.

'How right you are,' he murmured, smiling at her rigidity beneath his touch. 'Where were you going tonight?'

The tip of her tongue touched her upper lip. She wanted to look at him, but she knew what she would see, that merciless bronze mask enlivened only by eyes that glittered with contempt.

'Just to a party,' she said huskily. 'At the Stevensons'.'

'Then I'll take you.'

Christabel was shaking her head before he said the last word, 'No, it doesn't matter.'

'Why?' His hands slid up beneath her arms and came to rest with the knuckles pressed against her breasts, sending a shaft of electricity through her body.

Christabel flinched. 'No,' she said, the rawness of her throat reflected in her tones. 'It—I don't want to go.'

'Because I would be your escort?'

'Yes.' Hastily she added, 'I don't want to go without Nate.'

His fingers tightened on the firm flesh of her upper arms in a swift punishment for her rash challenge.

'A pity, but I'm quite determined to take you.' As she digested this, frowning, he added with a flick of the contempt which hurt her so, 'After all, it doesn't matter to you which man you go with, surely?'

And when she still didn't move he added with cool intent to hurt, 'I won't expect any recompense for my trouble, I promise you. Not even a goodnight kiss like the one you were so enthusiastically sharing last week.'

Christabel lifted her lashes, her gaze sliding up the tanned length of his throat to the angular line of jaw and the beautiful mouth, at once severe and sensuous, the clear-cut lips as sharply moulded as those of any statue.

She dared lift her eyes no farther. That hard mouth told her all she needed to know. For some reason, some unpleasant reason, he was going to make it impossible for her to stay away from the party. And although she hated him and despised herself she could feel heat suffusing her skin and the dragging ache of desire in the pit of her stomach.

'Very well,' she said in subdued tones, trying not to sound at all submissive.

'Good girl!' To any eavesdropper the words

expressed nothing more than a kind of casual acceptance, but Christabel's ears caught the hidden satisfaction beneath the even voice. 'Go and get ready. I'm leaving in half an hour.'

The Stevensons, Charlie and Sis, were an almost middle-aged couple with pretensions to social status somewhat alleviated by genuine kindness and a delight in entertaining. They greeted Christabel with interest and Alex with enthusiasm not unmixed with a certain smugness at having captured such a prize. Christabel's lethargy lifted for long enough to cast a fleeting, meaningful glance at him, only to meet wry laughter. He knew, but he also was too shrewd not to pick up their essential characters.

It was sweet to share such a joke; it was the only pleasant moment in an evening that rapidly turned into a nightmare. Penny was there, of course, trailing a young man whose face was vaguely familiar to Christabel. It was to become a lot more familiar to her, for Penny no sooner saw Alex's head above those around him than she arrived, round blue eyes speculative and measuring.

'Hi,' she said. 'Remember me?'

'How could I forget?' Alex's voice was warm and caressing with a note of laughter in the deep tones.

Penny smiled, obviously pleased. 'Well, quite easily, I'd imagine.' She introduced the young man, whose name was Steven someone, and homed into the attack again. 'Where's Nate?'

'Out on a call,' Christabel said quietly.

The enormous blue eyes swung from Christabel's carefully made up face to Alex's. What she saw there apparently pleased her, for she became expansive and all too soon it became only too clear that not only had she set her cap for Alex but that he was responding, flirting with her with all the urbane charm Christabel remembered so well, so that for all her air of sophistication Penny was soon pink-cheeked and dazzled, her eyes bright with a vivid excitement which made Christabel want to weep. On the night of Sarah's wedding that must have been how she looked, bemused into lowering her guard and with what disastrous results! It was to be hoped that Penny knew exactly what she was doing.

Several times Christabel moved away to speak to others, but each time they seemed to come together again until she obeyed a beckoning finger from across the room and left them to join Sis Stevenson who was enjoying the situation.

'Well, Penny certainly gets top marks for effort,' she began. 'Do you think someone should warn her that men as virile as Alex Thomassin usually don't expect just a goodnight kiss?'

'I should say she's well aware of the kind of man he is,' Christabel told her. It took an immense amount of effort to infuse her voice with just the right colouring of dry humour. Never in her life had she felt less like laughing, and she thanked her mother for persuading her to go into modelling. It had given her good experience in managing her expression.

So she smiled into Sis's slightly avid face and went on calmly, 'Anyway, Alex isn't stupid.'

Cruel, yes, ruthless and arrogant and totally cynical, but never stupid.

'No, although,' Sis said acidly, watching as one of their neighbours laughed too loudly at the joke made by his cousin's wife, 'some men would forget anything when confronted by a pretty face and a willing disposition.'

'You don't get to be where he is by allowing your desires to override caution,' Christabel observed with composure.

'Don't you like him?'

Clad in deep green velvet, Christabel's shoulders lifted in a shrug. 'Yes, he's very likeable. But I wouldn't like to cross him, and I certainly would never try to beat him in a business deal, or cheat him in any way or try to make a fool of him. Still, he's an immensely charismatic man.'

If Sis noticed the reservation behind the reply she said nothing. 'Well, you can always get the Garritys to give you a ride home,' she said practically, then flushed as she realised what she had said.

'So I can.' Anyone who didn't know Christabel well would have taken the small quiver in her voice to be one of amusement.

Sis certainly did. 'Well, you know what I mean,' she said comfortably. 'Come and talk to Rob. She's been trying to catch your eye for ten minutes.'

The first half of the evening was endurable, if only just. It took Christabel all of her will-power and stamina to move around the room, talking, smiling, behaving as though she hadn't a care in all the world, devoutly grateful to whoever had invented coloured make-up base and all the rest of the cosmetics which prevented her pallor from being blatantly obvious.

No, she got through the first part of the evening quite well. It wasn't until Charlie began showing off his enormous and expensive tape deck that things became unbearable. For he chose, of course, music to dance to, and the sight of Penny in Alex's arms, her face lifted to his in stunned fascination, made Chistabel feel as though she could curl up and die.

And there was nothing she could do, nothing except stop herself from forcibly tearing Penny free from him. Jealousy, acrid and burning, rode through her body in a tide like nausea. Not only was she jealous, she was fiercely, bitterly angry as though someone had stolen something of great worth to her, a necessary part of her existence. It was an emotion she had never felt before, not even when she had seen Greg with Fliss Thomassin. And the implications of this she was forced to face.

Because this was something else, a fierce burning possessiveness that racked like a physical pain. Oh, she thought, swaying gently to a dreamy tune with Steven Someone-or-other who had grown more and more sulky as Alex continued to monopolise Penny, oh God, I love him, the swine!

It had been inevitable, as inescapable as the fact of spring each year. In spite of the surface gloss of worldliness on her personality Christabel had always unconsciously been a seeker after love, yearning for the perfect lover even when her mother and common sense tried to convince her that there was no such thing. Companionship, Brenda had said often enough, and sex were all that could be expected from even the happiest marriage. Why expect bells to ring and lights to flash as well?

Such savage irony which had lured Christabel into loving the one man she could not have except in the most crude way!

The episode with Greg had been a practice run, a combination of physical attraction and the lingering carry-over of the years when she had despaired of living up to her mother. It had been sweet and extremely good for her self-respect when a clever, ambitious man made her think she was a suitable match for him. Greg had flattered and kissed her into dependence, but when she had been forced to realise that all he wanted from her was her body the love she thought so deep had melted away like a wave into sand.

And that was why, of course, she had been so—so *available* to the complex blend of sensuality and charisma which was Alex's public persona. Hurt and bewildered, she had needed comfort and his unabashed pursuit had provided that, but more than that, the initial impact of that overwhelming attraction had knocked her completely off balance.

Perhaps even then, in an odd way, she had loved him. At least she had realised that the potential for love was there.

That was why she had fought him so hard, been so

determined not to allow him through the defences she
had erected with such care. Greg's defection had
bruised her heart, but it had also hurt an equally
vulnerable area, her ego. And her surrender to passion
had further weakened her self-respect. Alex had been
right. To punish herself she had refused to accept that
there was anything more to their relationship than an
attraction which was degrading to her.

And her refusal to be anything other than guiltily
ashamed by it had angered him and made him cruel and
finally turned him off completely. He would go away,
and she would never know just what might have
eventuated if she had not hugged her guilt and shame so
firmly to herself and refused to relinquish it.

'Penny looks as though she's just been given the key
to Fort Knox,' said Sis, suddenly appearing from
behind when the tune finished and Steven went to get
them drinks. 'Oh well, she's not such an innocent. It
looks rather as though you'll be going home with the
Garritys, after all. He's certainly pouring on the charm,
isn't he.' She considered a moment, head to one side as
she watched the two of them, Alex towering over Penny
as he smiled down at her. 'Not that he does exactly turn
it on. It's always there, isn't it. He just turns the heat up
when he wants to.'

'Like a furnace,' Christabel agreed, trying to sound
amused.

'Well, let's hope Penny doesn't get too badly burned.
Now, here's Steven looking forlorn. I'm glad you're
taking pity on him, Kirsty.'

So she danced with him again and then with several
other men, did a parody of a tango with Ash Muirhead
that brought laughter and applause, and rather thought
that she was holding her head high enough for no one
to realise that she was racked by a bitter desolation.

For Alex and Penny seemed to be in a little world of
their own, totally absorbed in each other. It was so—so
deliberately done, exactly as he had isolated her on the

night of Sarah's wedding, cut her out of the crowd as if he was the hunter and she the prey.

The anger was partly at herself for having been so stupid as to fall in love with him and refuse to recognise it. But oh, it was bitter cold jealousy that darkened her eyes when she thought of Penny in his arms, lying with him in ecstasy before the night was over. And she knew that there would be no sleep for her; her imagination was so vivid that it would keep her awake until he got home, and then anger would take over so that by morning she would be a wreck.

And she would have to face him with Donald and Elaine looking on so that when she met his taunting eyes she would have to be calm and controlled, as poised as if she didn't want to kill him.

The intensity of her emotions horrified her, but she was unable to damp them down. It took all her self-command to keep her social mask firmly in place. However, she managed to do it, was even amused in a cynical way at how easy it was to fool people who had known her all her life.

Even when Nate appeared, kind, dependable, everything that Alex was not, she resisted the temptation to fly to him as though he was her saviour. But her smile was brilliantly warm as he bent and kissed her cheek, surveying her slender form in the long silk trousers and elaborate velvet jacket with open appreciation.

'You look lovely,' he said. 'Like something from someone's harem.'

'Something?'

He grinned. 'Chief concubine. Come and dance with me. I need a little light relief.'

'Oh?' She swayed into his arms, her eyes scanning his face anxiously. 'What happened?'

'We lost the bitch,' he said briefly.

'Oh, *Nate*, I'm so sorry!'

He turned his face into the hand that touched his

cheek in the age-old gesture of comfort. 'Never mind, it happens. Mary's upset, of course, but she'll have all the fun of choosing a new one.' His voice altered. 'Can you tell me why Alex Thomassin should have just sent me the sort of look that makes hair curl?'

Oh yes, nothing easier. Was there a taint of the dog in the manger in every man?

Aloud Christabel said lightly. 'I think you must have mistaken it. He's very interested in Penny, as you see.'

'What I see is Penny very interested in him. He's giving nothing away. Handsome devil, isn't he, but a proper poker-player's face. Do you like him?'

That was the second time tonight she had been asked the question. Now, with the discovery of her own true feelings towards him she couldn't airily answer as she had to Sis.

'Not much,' she said quietly. 'Oh, he's charming, but that's pure stone beneath.'

'Elaine and Donald are very impressed with him.'

She nodded, with difficulty keeping her eyes from the couple on the other side of the room. 'They're no more immune to his charm than—than poor Penny over there. That first time he came up he set out to make himself pleasant. When we found out about the development Dad couldn't bring himself to object because by then he liked him immensely.'

'And you?' Nate asked quietly. 'Did you like him, Kirsty?'

In a way it was a relief. Nate knew, of course, had probably known ever since Alex came to Rangitatau; he was astute enough to notice the difference in her.

She lifted her head, met his concerned gaze directly. 'No,' she said baldly.

'I'd guessed not,' he murmured, sliding both arms around her to hug her, returning the comfort she had offered him. 'Poor Kirsty! But you'll get over him, you know. You have spirit and courage and strength. I suppose everyone has to fall for someone totally unsuitable once in their life.'

Something in his voice made her stop biting her lip and look up at him. 'You?'

He smiled, but there was something bleak in it. 'Oh, yes.'

'Not——?'

'No, not you.' His arms tightened before he released her into a more conventional hold. 'No, I find you eminently suitable, Kirsty. My love is so far out of sight that there's no hope for me.'

She sighed, picking up the meaning in his use of the present tense. So much for her fears that he might be too fond of her! Oh Vanity, thy name is woman, she thought drily before saying with impulsive affection. 'I can't imagine anyone who would be out of your reach, Nate! Don't be defeatist—go out there and get her!'

He laughed at that, wryly. 'It's not that easy, my dear. Unfortunately she's not only out of reach, there's just no possibility that we'll get together. But why not you? Don't tell me you couldn't attract him away from Penny if you wanted to, because I won't believe you.'

'It's not that simple,' she mimicked, her smile twisted on her lips. 'Now, let's forget, shall we, and just enjoy ourselves.'

CHAPTER ELEVEN

BRAVE words, and on Christabel's part anyway, doomed to be unfulfilled. Still, it was much better to have Nate with her giving his unstinting support, especially when Penny and Alex joined them.

It was agony to see Penny curved into Alex's side, his arm about her shoulders as she gazed up into his face. An even greater agony was the quick, merciless glance that scorched across towards Christabel. Her eyes closed in a momentary spasm of defence, but she recognised the coldly sardonic satisfaction she glimpsed before Alex's lashes in turn came down and he bent his head to smile at Penny.

He knew exactly what he was doing and he was enjoying watching her squirm like a fish on a line, hooked through the heart. This was her punishment for refusing him.

A fragment of poetry floated through her brain. The Song of Solomon had said it all, thousands of years ago: *'Love is as strong as death; jealousy is as cruel as the grave.'*

Within Nate's warm clasp her hand trembled. His fingers tightened. 'Like a drink?' he asked quietly.

'Yes—yes, please.' Anything to occupy her hands, to give her something else to think about.

'Aren't you feeling well?' Penny asked solicitously. 'You look a bit pale beneath that superb make-up, Kirsty. Don't you think so, Alex?'

Nate had turned away; he stopped and looked at Penny for a moment before continuing on his errand.

'Somewhere in Christabel's cold heart a spark of warmth was ignited. Nate might not love her, but he cared, and at the moment she needed any sort of support she could find.

Alex's voice was amused as his hand came out and tilted Christabel's face towards him, his scrutiny thorough and relentless. 'Tired, Christabel?'

'Not in the least,' she returned with a cool composure which was only betrayed by a swift flick of her lashes and the slow draining of colour from her skin.

Beside him, still held by his other arm, Penny stirred restlessly. As he released Christabel the high, deliberately childish voice observed with a petulance which showed how much her conquest had gone to her head, 'It must have been the light that made you look a bit haggish, I suppose. Alex, why do you call her Christabel? It's such a *contrived*, pretentious name—I'm sure she'd far rather be known as Kirsty, wouldn't you, Kirsty?'

It was easy enough to shrug. 'I've no preference.'

But Alex said smoothly, 'I like it. It suits her. Haven't you read Coleridge's poem, Penny?'

'No.' Penny opened her eyes to their widest extent. 'Is it a real name, then? I always thought it was made-up. As for Coleridge—well, I'm afraid I'm not a very intellectual person. I'm better on action.'

The heavy note of meaning underlined the implicit promise in her words. She stared defiantly at Christabel.

But Christabel could not be hurt by Penny. On the night they had met Alex had teased her about her name; he was using Penny's little dig to hammer home the reality of his decision, underlining the connection between the two, as if she needed reminding!

Sudden sympathy for the triumphant Penny hurt her. If she had thought it would do any good she would have tried to warn her, but one glance at the smug pretty face dissuaded her. Penny would laugh at her, accuse her of jealousy and envy.

Where was Nate? Christabel risked a quick look around which revealed Nate bailed up by their hostess.

He was too well mannered to cut her short, so she could expect little help from him for a while.

'You know, you do look tired. Or unhappy.' Penny reverted to the topic with her normal nagging persistence. 'Perhaps you should have an early night. There's quite a nasty 'flu going round. You might be coming down with it.'

All of a sudden Christabel was sick of everything, sick of Penny and her innuendoes, sick of Alex's cruelty, but most of all sick of the effort needed to keep her pride intact.

'You could be right,' she said. 'So if you'll excuse me . . .' Against her will her glance was dragged across to the man who was watching her through narrowed eyes.

As she spoke he straightened up, removing his arm from around Penny's shoulders. 'Get your wrap,' he said, incredibly. 'I'll meet you by the door.'

If she had been as vindictive as Penny Christabel would have enjoyed the astounded fury which spread over that pretty face as the meaning of his words sank in.

As smoothly as if he hadn't spent all night dazzling her into submission he continued, 'Now where's that—oh, there he is. What's his name? Steven someone.'

'But—but *Alex*——!' Penny stopped precipitately, warned to silence by something austere in the handsome face which bent enquiringly towards her.

'He was the one who brought you here, wasn't he?'

'I—yes.'

'Then naturally you'll be going home with him.'

Christabel's compassionate heart was wrung by Penny's complete loss of face.

In the car she said heavily, 'My God, you're a bastard.'

'But a polite one,' he said with cool insolence. 'My mother always told me that it was the height of ill manners to go home with a different girl from the one I took.'

'Why? *Why* did you do it? I thought——' she stopped, flushing.

In the quiet darkness of the car his sideways glance was like a whip. 'I know what you thought,' he said pleasantly enough. 'You were wrong, as you usually are. She might think twice before abandoning her escort with such enthusiasm next time. How do you think he felt, watching her flirt all evening with me? She couldn't have cared less about the poor guy.'

'You did exactly the same to me,' she pointed out, not seeing until too late how foolish the comparison was.

'Ah, but we're conducting our own private little war, aren't we, darling. And all's fair there.'

Hastily she changed tack, uneasy at the jeering undertone in the smooth voice. 'So you deliberately set her up before all her friends! That was a cruel thing to do.'

'She's a cruel little cat. It's time someone showed her what it's like to be on the receiving end.' His voice was dispassionate. It could not have been clearer that he had no feeling at all for Penny, not liking, not respect, not even desire in spite of all of her efforts to attract it.

Christabel shivered. 'I still think it was a rotten thing to do. You made her look an absolute fool.'

'Why should you care? She didn't worry about the boy she came with, or, if it comes to that, about you.' He shot another piercing glance her way. 'Tender-hearted little soul, aren't you?'

Reacting to the sneer, she said defensively, 'She can't help being the way she is.'

'I happen to think you're wrong. Anyone can change if they want to. It's just a matter of working at it.'

A counsel of perfection indeed, she thought bitterly. Probably he could use his immense will-power to change those parts of his character he disliked, but lesser mortals had to put up with the personality their heredity and environment formed.

'If you say so,' she said tonelessly. 'Myself, I'd have thought that humiliating her was hardly the best way to go about it. But you're an expert at that, aren't you?'

'When have I humiliated you?'

Almost she gasped, but caution warned her that she had steered the conversation into dangerous paths. Aloud she muttered, 'Oh, forget it. It doesn't matter.'

Apparently he was going to let her get away with it, because he made no reply. Huddled into her wrap, she watched with dull eyes as night's landscape flashed by. Because the road was still being reconstructed he was unable to go really fast, but the big car was kept at the limit of safety and several times she was grateful for the safety belt. It was unlike him to drive so fast; she sighed. He was angry, as angry as she was.

Although there was no moon to light the way the sky was clear so that starshine lent its cool, dim, deceptive glamour to the scenery.

At the approach to the remaining untouched bridge he slowed, saying as the planks rattled beneath the car, 'What time do your parents expect you home?'

'No time,' she answered slowly, startled. 'I'm a big girl now.'

'Then in that case,' he said through teeth that snapped together, 'we'll stop a while and sort a few things out, shall we?' and spun the wheel to put them on to the grassy verge.

'There's nothing to sort out,' she protested swiftly, too swiftly to be able to hide the fear in her voice.

As he cut the engine he said, the very quietness of the words emphasising their ominous undertone, 'Oh yes, there is. Let's start with the handsome vet, shall we? Does it hurt to know that he's not in love with you?'

Thoughts chased around her head in frantic confusion. Outside, their presence must have startled a cock pheasant, for he called loudly and they could hear the whir of his wings as he flew to cover in a row of hakea trees.

'No, it doesn't hurt,' she said, half beneath her breath. She had to say something. He was sitting with his hands still on the wheel as though he didn't trust himself to relax them. She could feel the tension in him, the desire to hurt and knew with a fatalistic certainty that he wouldn't hesitate to shake the truth from her if he thought it necessary.

'You did know?'

'Yes.' A little more strongly she continued, 'I'm very fond of Nate. He's kind and thoughtful and fun——'

'Oh, spare me a recital of his virtues,' he interrupted nastily. For a moment his fingers drummed on the wheel until, as if the involuntary movement was a betrayal, the sound ceased.

'Right,' he said calmly, 'so that disposes of him. Now about my expertise at humiliation. When did I humiliate you?'

'I said it didn't matter.'

'You said so, I didn't. Was it when I asked you to be my mistress?'

Silence. She sat still, refusing to move.

Very softly he said, 'I don't really care how long I have to sit here or exactly what methods I use to chisel the truth from your incredibly thick mind. So,' his voice dropped a note, 'how about telling me?'

'I'm not—it doesn't matter,' she retorted stonily, hands clenched in her lap as she kept her head rigidly set on shoulders which ached with the tension.

She heard the swift harsh intake of his breath, but even as he turned towards her lights appeared from behind and a car swept past with a derisive toot on the horn.

And he laughed under his breath and switched the engine on, keeping it idling until the dust settled. 'How wrong can you be?' he asked elliptically as he set the car in motion.

But as they ran into the garage he said with cold determination, 'We've only postponed this discussion,

Christabel, not cancelled it. So don't go getting any ideas.'

She rubbed her eyes with the back of her hand and he said impatiently, 'Oh, get off to bed! You look like a kid that's too tired to sleep.'

So apparently he didn't plan to pursue the discussion then. The next day Christabel found out why.

'Well, we've got to go.' Elaine spoke firmly, then smiled a coaxing little smile at her husband. 'Darling, you know Phyllis and I arranged it and you agreed.'

Donald sighed heavily before addressing himself to Alex across the breakfast table, 'When you're married,' he said, 'don't ever let your wife ask you anything just before you go to sleep. You forget, but she doesn't.'

Alex grinned at him. 'I'll remember that,' he promised.

'O.K.,' said Donald in a martyred voice. 'I'll take you to spend the day at Phyllis Sergeant's place provided I'm allowed to help Len do his stock rounds.'

Elaine laughed and shook her fist at him, but agreed before asking, 'What about you, Alex? Didn't you say you had a meeting?'

'A gaggle of Members of Parliament,' he agreed somewhat wearily. He looked tired, that splendid virility a little dimmed as though he had, like Christabel, spent most of the preceding night awake.

The ravages of her sleepless night were covered with make-up, but there was no such option for a man. For the first time Christabel looked straight at him, met the cool enquiry in his glance and flushed.

'Fun for you,' she observed lightly, tackling her grapefruit.

'It has to be done. They'll want to have a good look around, but I'll be back in time for dinner.'

Almost she heaved a sigh of relief. At least she wouldn't be left here alone with him.

'Well, you'll have a good day for it,' Donald commented. He cast an experienced eye out of the window. 'Good morning, anyway. It looks as though it might close in this afternoon. Forecast's for rain and wind.' He frowned, staring abstractedly at the toast he was about to eat. 'Oh yes, before I forget. Might be a good idea, Alex, to warn your men that although Rangitatau looks like paradise it can turn nasty. Yesterday I noticed a couple of chaps fishing from the rocks at the base of the north Gate. They'll be quite safe there until the weather blows up, but you have to know your spot then.'

Alex nodded. 'I'll see they're warned,' he said briefly. 'Still a ban on rabbit shooting?'

'Most of them would be quite responsible, I know,' Donald agreed. 'But my stock is valuable. It only needs one idiot to lose me a thousand dollars or so.'

'Fair enough.' Alex didn't offer to make good any losses; he obviously had some idea of the ramifications of the sort of breeding policy which Donald followed. Money was no replacement for a carefully bred beast.

Christabel sipped her coffee slowly. She knew that although the construction workers toiled long hours which left them with little time for relaxation they needed something to occupy them in the time they did have. Many fished, some went to the nearest hotel and made use of its instant fellowship, a few were finding their feet in the social life of the district. Sally Kitts, at the garage was dreamily enamoured of one of the younger men, a pleasant, fair giant who was making a name for himself in the rugby team.

'Why not ask the manager of the Lands and Surveys Development if they can shoot over the Waipouri Block?' she asked diffidently. 'I know there are rabbits there. Nate and I rode down to the lagoon and the sandbanks there are infested with them.'

'That's an idea.' Donald eyed his daughter approvingly before turning to Alex. 'You know it, it's about six miles back down the road. It was brought in about twenty years ago and then let go back, but the department isn't doing anything to it yet. John Garrity is a reasonable chap, he'd probably be quite pleased to have someone try to get the numbers down.'

'I'll get it organised.' Alex asked coolly, 'Just for interest, why doesn't the presence of rabbits worry you?'

'Kirsty and I keep them down,' Donald told him. 'There aren't that many. The ones your men see are those they've disturbed with all that earth-moving.' He looked up as Élaine bustled back into the room. 'Just about ready, are you?'

'There's just the dishes.'

'I'll do them,' Christabel offered, jumping to her feet, more than a little glad at the excuse to get away from Alex's presence.

Half an hour later she had the house to herself, peaceful and quiet with only the ever-present growl of the construction machines to spoil the atmosphere.

Slowly, dreamily, she did the dishes and tidied the house, then renewed all the flowers and stood for a long minute outside the door to Alex's room with a bowl of jonquils in her hands. It was stupid to feel this way, but she couldn't rid herself of the conviction that by going into it she was putting herself into danger.

'Don't be a fool,' she said aloud, and pushed the door open.

It was immaculately tidy, the bed already made, the desk top a gleaming, empty expanse. Only the presence of brushes on the dressing table revealed that it was not unoccupied. That, and a book on the night table. Curiosity, enhanced by a yearning to know even a little more about him than she did, brought her across to read the title. The Odyssey, that story of the arch-trickster Odysseus' journey home to his faithful wife Penelope.

It seemed an odd choice for such a sophisticated man, a story of high romance and barbarism, of low cunning and heroic deeds, yet as she touched the well-thumbed pages she could imagine him relaxing with wily Odysseus and the sonorous cadences of Homer's poetry.

Suddenly she seemed to pry. She put the jonquils on the bureau and left the room, biting her lip to control the sudden rush of anguish.

Not much longer. He must leave soon, and when he did she would leave too, go down to Auckland and find work, any sort of work to keep her brain and body occupied so that she wouldn't be tormented by this aching hollowness which kept her awake at night and spoiled the days.

Love denied must fade, must die, surely. Nowadays no one died of love or waited for the perfect lover. No, better by far to pick herself up and try again, and this time not let physical attraction blind her until it was too late.

'That's twice you've made a fool of yourself,' she said as she pulled a packet of frozen fillet steak from the freezer. 'Third time lucky, girl.'

But she was whistling in the wind, and she knew it.

After lunch, an apple and an orange washed down by a cup of coffee, she made her way to a part of the garden hidden from any casual eyes and lay on a rug, head pillowed in her arms while the sun beat down on her. And if she cried a little no one knew or heard her.

It was a chill in the weather which brought her, shivering, upright. The clouds Donald had predicted had arrived.

Yawning, headachy, she picked up the rug and walked slowly across the lawn. The sky was ominous, a great line of cloud approaching low, almost stealthily creeping up on Rangitatau. Rain and wind indeed! It was going to be a proper storm.

For the next few minutes she dashed around closing windows and latching doors, bringing in the deck chairs and outdoor furniture, while the cloud grew inexorably, a hard bar of black overwhelming the paler, higher clouds which had preceded it.

At the first lash of rain she was running from the hen-house, only a few yards away from the house, but the wind grabbed her mercilessly and by the time she reached the porch she was drenched and gasping, for the rain was icy.

As she towelled herself dry she found herself wondering mirthlessly if the Members of Parliament had got their inspection over and done with.

Almost it seemed as though her thoughts had summoned their subject, for Alex's car belted across the cattlestop and into the garage, and before she had time to realise that she was gaping, blouse and shorts in wet heaps at her feet with only a towel to cover her, he was in through the door, his brilliant eyes flashing the length of her body in one sweeping all-seeing glance which returned to linger on her face, pale and defiant beneath the wet strands of hair.

'Hurry up and dry yourself,' he said curtly. 'You're all gooseflesh,' and he brushed past her into the house.

Well, he couldn't have made his lack of interest any more obvious. Still with the towel draped around her, she ran along to her bedroom and finished the job, hauling a pair of corduroy jeans and a thick warm jersey over a blouse of fine wool. Trembling fingers combed her hair into its usual smooth cap before she re-applied lip gloss.

Then, squaring her shoulders, she made her way to the little parlour.

He was kneeling by the fireplace, broad shoulders almost blocking out the sight of the leaping flames above the kindling. When he heard her he turned and got up, his expression that self-contained mask she knew so well, the hooded eyes assessing her face with keen purpose.

'And now,' he said, the quiet words a threat, 'we have a conversation to resume.'

'What about your M.P.s?' she asked desperately.

'Gone.'

'But you said——' She stopped, remembering exactly what he had said, the devious swine.

'That I'd be back in time for dinner. Quite correct—I am. If I'd let you realise that they had an appointment for lunch farther up the coast you'd have gone with your parents.' He gestured towards a chair. 'Sit down, Christabel. There are no people around to interrupt us, no cars to toot, nothing to stop us from finishing our discussion of last night. I want to find out what makes you tick and I have every intention of doing just that.'

'You want to dissect me like—like a frog in a lab,' she said bitterly, not moving.

He grinned. 'Just that, my lovely. I find the workings of your mind totally and completely fascinating. I promised myself that I'm not going to leave here this time without discovering how the hell your personal computer can process the data it's given and come up with the peculiarly slanted reactions that pass for attitudes with you.'

He wasn't joking, although the words were cast in a humorous mould. Christabel looked at him, met steely determination and stood, irresolute.

'We can do it one of two ways,' he observed pleasantly. 'Like this—or I can take you off to my bedroom and extract the truth from you there. That's my personal favourite of the alternatives, but the decision is yours.'

'You wouldn't——' She stopped precipitately.

'Just try me.'

A gust of wind thrummed viciously against the windows. Christabel stared at the man opposite, recognised his implacable determination and surrendered to it, bitterly angry with herself for her subjugation. 'I'll never forgive you,' she said between her teeth as she walked across to the chair he indicated.

Before she sat down something caught her eye. Her head whipped around to the window as she strained her eyes to penetrate the murk outside. Momentarily the rain had stopped, but the bay was a mass of heaving white-caps, grey and threatening, whipped up by the vicious gusts of wind.

'Look,' she said sharply, pointing.

'What——?' He stopped, because he too had seen what she had seen. 'Get me some binoculars,' he ordered between his teeth.

She raced into the morning room and snatched the binoculars from the bookshelf. It took her a moment to adjust the lenses, her hands were trembling so, but one sweep revealed what her eyes had caught. Out there in that maelstrom, in a small, frail aluminium dinghy a man was struggling desperately for his life.

Seconds later the binoculars were dragged forcibly from her. As Alex put them to his eyes she turned and ran towards the porch. A moment later he joined her.

'You'd better ring the camp,' she said quickly, dragging on her waterproof parka. 'Tell them to——'

'Just a minute!' His hand on her arm was steel-strong. 'Where the hell do you think you're going?'

She met his eyes impatiently. 'To get him, of course. I'll take the boat out.'

'Don't be a fool!'

'I'll have to.' She tried to wriggle free from his restraining grip, every nerve and muscle stretched. 'Alex, he's not going to last much longer in that dinghy. Someone's got to get him, and I know the bay like the back of my hand. He's already inside the first lot of rocks—if he's not picked up soon he's going to end up smashed on to the reef.'

He swore softly and savagely, but he let her go, only to haul Donald's oilskins over his head. 'You can't manage the launch by yourself,' he said roughly.

She felt an unaccountable lift to her heart. 'We can't take the launch.' She spoke urgently as she fastened the heavy, slick plastic of her jacket. 'It's too big to take in among those rocks. It will have to be the runabout.'

Smaller and less seaworthy, so increasing the danger to all of them.

Beneath his tan Alex had gone pale and after she had spoken he closed his eyes momentarily. Then he nodded and bent his head and kissed her fiercely, crushing her mouth beneath so that the salt taste of blood spurted on to her tongue.

'Come on,' he commanded tersely.

It would have taken her three times as long to get there by herself. After she had rung the camp to warn them she ran down through the rain and wind and found him waiting in the runabout, the big outboard ticking over.

Once she was in Alex gunned the engines and took them out across the bay far faster than she would ever have dared, his face taut with concentration beneath the lash of the rain.

Confidence flooded through her, reinforcing the boost given by the adrenalin in her blood. When they neared the first reef she touched his arm, slid in front of him and took the wheel, frowning, her bottom lip clenched in her teeth as she fought the wheel through the short steep waves.

Ahead lay a white, surging mass of water broken only by the menacing outlines of the rocks. Rain and spume dashed into her face so that she had to blink fiercely to keep her eyes clear, her slender hands steady as she brought the fragile little craft ever nearer and nearer to the reef.

The fisherman had chosen his spot well, a pool among a maze of reefs which partly protected him from the full force of the waves. In fine weather no more ideal position could be found.

Now it revealed itself to be a trap. There was only one safe entrance, a narrow alley between the rocks and that was hardly safe now for waves broke and surged and jostled there, preventing such a frail little craft from forcing a passage back out. Already the dinghy had overturned, bobbing like a strange bird on the water, while its occupant, clad in a red jacket and long, dangerously clinging trousers, was being washed inexorably towards the seething, jagged rocks.

For an intuitive moment Christabel could feel his fear, the gnawing weakness, the life force ebbing in this maelstrom of wind and weather.

Very carefully, unconsciously praying, she eased the bow towards the reef so that the engines were protected from damage on the rocks. Alex didn't even look at her as he picked up the coil of rope.

She had chosen the spot carefully, using the small bulk of the runabout to give some protection from the full force of the waves to the feebly swimming man in the water. Now she kept them in place as the rope sang out across the grey and white waters.

Thank God the man still had feeling in his hands! For the frightening few moments that it took for him to scramble the loop over his shoulders Christabel's mouth formed unspoken encouragement to hurry, please hurry, while she watched the waves that threatened them all.

Meanwhile Alex paid out the rope until she felt the tug against the hull and knew he was beginning to haul the man in.

He was a big man, rendered even bulkier by the thick jacket he wore, sodden now and clearly weighing him down. But Alex made short work of hauling him inboard, dragging him over the side with a strength which awed her even as she used her weight and the throttle to trim the boat.

And then Alex yelled, 'O.K., take her out!'

If anything it was even trickier going back through the reefs. Christabel had to fight down the impulse that urged her to open the throttle and get as far away from the danger as possible, concentrating with such fierce purpose that she bit through her lip.

But at last they were free and out into the bigger but much less dangerous waves.

'Right,' Alex said curtly, not even looking at the man he had rescued as he shouldered her aside to take the wheel.

She staggered but caught at the coaming, just managing to keep her feet as the sound of the engine rose into a deep roar. The runabout bounced across the waves with a series of thuds that made her wince.

'We won't be long now!' she shouted at the fisherman who was huddled in the bottom of the boat, grey and exhausted.

He lifted his head and produced a weak smile, but was unable to sustain it because of the incessant shivers that shook him. Christabel knew enough to be thankful for those shivers. They were a good sign. Exposure had barely set in.

When she straightened up he collapsed back against the coaming, his eyes closing again. He was not young, and for anxious moments Christabel wondered if he had damaged his heart.

She was shaking too, long rigours which were just a reaction to stress. Although the rain had eased the wind still tore at her face which, paradoxically, felt as though the outer layer of skin had been scalded. Exhausted by the surge of adrenalin which had kept her concentration high, she was racked by weariness and an intense depression. The combination of rain and spray had forced water in beneath her hood. Its clammy chill spread all across her back and arms and down to her breasts.

Beside her Alex could have been a statue carved of some dark, glistening stone, the only moving parts his hands and arms as he brought the little craft in across the quieter waters of the homestead bay where the camp manager waited with a group of men, the first-aid team.

'I rang the hospital,' he told Alex, watching as the rescued man was carried up and placed gently on to a stretcher. 'We've got to get him warm and then take him in. They'll check him over.'

'Do you want to warm him at the homestead?' Christabel asked, shivering.

Alex answered for him, his voice abrasive. 'No, there's a perfectly good first aid room at the camp.'

'Thank you, Miss Grieves,' the camp manager said, smiling briefly at her.

She nodded and turned to watch the men who now unfurled two umbrellas over the stretcher, gay golf umbrellas, one in green and white stripes, the other an eye-shattering orange.'

Behind her Alex spoke in swift, incisive tones.

I should go up to the house, she thought tiredly, and change. Another shiver hit her so hard that she had to clench her teeth to stop them chattering. Her hands felt hot and swollen and stiff; she made them into fists and stuffed them into the pockets of her parka.

From the corner of her eye she caught the manager's nod just before he set off up the track after his men.

As she made to follow something flicked at the edge of her mind. She turned, realising with a weariness which was mainly reaction that the runabout would have to be attended to. Her legs ached as she turned back towards the beach.

'What—oh, I see.' Alex helped her haul the boat in to the shore. Without the need for speech they dragged it well above the tide line and left it there, but Alex took the outboard motor and carried it back to the boatshed and Christabel went with him, her brain oddly mushy so that it refused to function.

CHAPTER TWELVE

'COME on,' Alex ordered brusquely. 'You look as though you're the one with exposure.'

But he took her hand, apparently not caring in the least that his men might notice. Not that it was that sort of handclasp. For some reason he was angry; Christabel could feel the tension emanating from him, and when she stumbled he muttered something jerking her upright again with an unnecessary amount of force.

Once inside he said harshly, 'Get dry.'

Flushed, furious, Christabel hauled her parka over her head. It was awkward, but her hands were too numb to deal with the fastenings. He was disposing of Donald's oilskins with his usual deftness and as she stood shivering demanded her parka with an imperious jerk of his head.

'I'll hang them in the garage,' he said curtly, then, realising her inability to unfasten it, muttered and came across and practically tore the thing off her.

So he was angry. That made two of them. And the porch floor was dripping wet, a fine welcome home for Elaine. Muttering mild oaths beneath her breath, Christabel found a mop and began to wipe the floor.

'What the *hell* do you think you're doing?'

The question, delivered in molten tones, jerked her upright. Alex had stripped to the waist and was standing in the doorway to the garage, looking at her with such fury that she took an involuntary step backwards, the inside of her mouth dry.

'Cleaning up,' she retorted, pushing the mop across the floor to give emphasis to her answer.

'Get inside and put some clothes on,' he ordered. 'Haven't you any common sense at all?'

176

Christabel's head lifted defiantly. 'Just because I'm not as brilliant as the great Alex Thomassin it doesn't mean that I have to be——'

She was behaving childishly, but Alex's reaction took her totally by surprise. 'That's it!' he exclaimed, and came across the porch in a rush, jerking her over his shoulder in the classic sack-of-potatoes hold.

For a moment she was literally speechless with shock. Only for a moment, however.

'Put me down!' she yelled, trying to lever herself upwards. 'Oh, you beast, put me down or I'll—I'll——!'

'Shut up,' he muttered between his teeth. 'I've had it with you, right up to my neck. For once, you tormenting, tantalising little witch, you're going to do as I want you to, and there is absolutely no way you're going to get out of *this*!'

Just what he had in mind by *this* she didn't dare think, but as he spoke he had headed past her bedroom door.

'Oh, don't you dare!' she wailed, anger and fear strong enough to put a telltale tremble in her voice.

'I'll dare what I bloody well want!' he snapped as he turned into his bedroom.

'No, Alex—*please*!'

'Yes.' He spoke through gritted teeth and dumped her on to the bed, then ripped her clothes from her, holding her with casual, contemptuous ease while she fought, her nails raking his shoulder.

'Let me *go*!' she gasped frantically. He did just that, watching as she scrabbled for the sheet while his hands went to his belt.

'*No!*'

Terror drove her from the bed, but one hand grabbed a handful of hair and a moment later she was back on the bed again. Alex followed her down on to it, his expression so grim that fear kicked like a live thing in the pit of her stomach.

'I loathe you!' she wept, but he smiled, a slow, savage

baring of teeth and parted her legs with only a fraction of his strength and forced himself on her.

And discovered, as only then did she, that there was no need for force. The body had its own immutable laws, and although Christabel despised herself for it, hers wanted this man and this man only and took him sweetly and rapturously within itself so that he groaned something deep in his throat and the harshness of a moment ago fled.

He had certainly intended to hurt her. But that was forgotten now, and he held her for long moments until she stopped crying and lay resistless. Then he moved, slowly, using every ounce of experience gained in so many encounters like this, and she moved with him, her hatred repressed as her senses betrayed her mind once more. Whatever she thought, whatever justification her brain could produce for her hating him, her body would have none of it. From the first there had been an attraction between them which, for her, had developed into fetters as strong as any made of iron or steel.

If Alex wanted her to be his mistress she would say no, but he had only to touch her and her body said yes, and now he knew it.

'Oh, God, Christabel,' he muttered, and then there was nothing else but unbidden, unwanted ecstasy that rocketed them both into realms so far beyond what had ever happened before that all else faded in the rapture of the moment.

And with that indescribable loveliness came peace and a kind of profound gratitude which kept her silent as he bowed his head on to her breasts, his arms still locked tightly around her.

'We can't keep doing this,' he sighed against her damp skin. 'Sooner or later you're going to get pregnant. I think we'd better get married.'

Christabel's breath froze in her throat. 'What—*what* did you say?'

Alex looked up into her face, the glaze of surfeited

passion still smouldering deep in his eyes but overlaid by the mocking amusement she knew so well. 'You heard,' he said coolly, and put up a hand to smooth back the wet elf-locks which curled around her face.

'Did—were you hit on the head?'

A wry smile twisted his mouth. 'No, my darling, I'm in possession of all my senses.'

'But you don't believe in marriage!'

'I don't believe in love either, but if I'm not in love with you then I've discovered an entirely new set of emotions which defies description.' The hand which had been pushing back her hair moved slowly to trace her brows, touch the straight line of her nose, her mouth's sultry outline. 'I think you'd better marry me,' he continued as she stared at him in utter astonishment. 'I can't trust myself with you, and your father is too old-fashioned to like the idea of us living together.'

'I think—you're mad!'

Irony gleamed in the dark depths of his eyes. 'Mad for you,' he agreed readily, following his fingers with tantalising soft kisses. 'What did you do that first night? Cast a spell on me? One virgin sacrifice and I was a goner. Do you know I spent hours trying to coax your whereabouts from Sarah? She wouldn't tell me—just said that you needed a breathing space. God, when I saw you in that shop I——'

'*What?*' Somehow her hands had become entangled in the rain-darkened hair. She had been exploring the proud contours of his head, delighting in the crispness of his hair, the warmth rising from his skin. Now her fingers clenched and she jerked his head back. '*What* did you say?'

Laughter gleamed beneath the heavy lashes, laughter and mockery and desire. 'Didn't you realise it? Such an innocent you are, my lovely lady Christabel! Of course I recognised you. Everything about you, the clean, lovely lines of your body, the cool summery little voice, the way you move—oh, I'd had plenty of long lonely nights to remember the sight and feel and scent of you, your warmth and the way you responded with such innocent ardour in my bed. You'd haunted my dreams, made sex with anyone else totally unsatisfying—I remembered you, all right.'

There was enough menace in his voice for her to blink nervously at him, her hands stilled. 'But you told me—you said it took a while, that time after we found out what you were planning to do to the bay.'

'Ah, because I was hunting, and the first thing a good hunter learns is not to frighten his prey. If you'd known I recognised you instantly you'd have realised that it was because I saw you with more than just my eyes. My body recognised yours, even though all I saw was your back. And although I still hadn't faced all of the implications of that instant recognition, I knew that it would terrify you to know of it.'

Oh, he understood her too well. Of course she would have been repelled by his cold-blooded pursuit.

The menace was definitely there and the touch of his hands was no longer a caress; he was imposing ownership on her, showing her as he cupped the high peak of her breast that she was helpless beneath his strength.

Christabel made the mistake of resisting. Instantly his head swooped and he crushed her mouth beneath his while that relentless hand swept from breast to stomach, then to hip and thigh.

'*Don't!*' she gasped when she could, shamed because all that was untamed in her rose to meet his suddenly savage hunger.

'It's too late for that, my lovely. It was too late ten minutes after we met. In fact, if I'd had the wit to realise it, it was too late when I undressed you with my eyes in front of a restaurant full of people the night you were out dining with that puppy, Greg Bardsley.'

She refused to answer, staring at him with impotent anger while he laughed down into her face, his own dark and dangerous, teeth white as he bent and bit her shoulder, not very gently.

'I liked what I saw with my mind's eye that night,' he murmured, appreciating the shudder his action caused. 'But I was angry, because Fliss wanted Greg. I thought you were his mistress. So when I saw you at the wedding I decided to put you out of commission.'

Christabel froze, her lips forming a question she dared not ask. Now there was no laughter in the eyes that met hers, nothing but a sombre intensity she was forced to accept.

Slowly his hands came up to cup her face. She could feel the faint trembling of his fingers against her heated skin, was hit by a great surge of answering emotion.

'But instead of the hard, promiscuous woman I'd expected, you were sweet and far from sophisticated,' he said. 'And although up until that moment when I had you like a sleepy nymph in my bed I'd had every intention of making love to you, I knew I couldn't do it.'

'Until I turned out to be wanton as well as sleepy,' she said slyly.

He nodded, kissing her eyes shut, his voice deep and profound. 'Then of course, you proved to be a very virginal nymph, and although I was shattered I couldn't help but be pleased. When I drove you home that night I was looking forward with a considerable amount of relish to initiating you into all the joys and mysteries of sex.'

'But you were beastly to me, accusing me of— wanting to get pregnant to you so that I could live off you!'

'Mm, I know.' Alex laughed softly at her indignation. 'A rearguard action, believe me. That should have warned me. The thought of you pregnant with my child wasn't at all distasteful.'

He moved down her body, adoring it, until his open mouth touched the flat plane of her stomach, his hands shaping the contours where their child would rest, his lips sensuous yet tender.

Christabel touched the wide line of his shoulder, smoothing across the skin, the tips of her fingers thrilling to the bunched strength of the muscles beneath. To her he was perfect physically, his body by some mysterious alchemy attuned to hers so that together they found a passionately complete fulfilment. Yet for him there had been others, other women who must have given him the same erotic satisfaction.

A bleakness made itself felt around the region of her heart. He looked up, suddenly alert, like the hunter he had likened himself to.

'What is it, my heart?'

At first she shook her head, not realising until then just how much she loved him; the thought of him locked in the same abandoned embrace with any other woman but her made her cold with jealousy and pale with desolation and hot with anger.

It was uncanny how he understood her, his expression wryly sympathetic as he moved up beside her and scooped her to lie with her head against his chest in the age-old position of comfort.

'I could promise you my complete fidelity, along with the moon and the stars and a galaxy or two, but it all amounts to trust,' he said quietly. 'I love you, Christabel. I can't imagine making love to anyone else, because since that first night you've been the sum of all women for me, the ideal one. At first I thought it was solely physical, that somehow I'd stumbled on the one woman whose body was the perfect other. But when I couldn't find you I realised it was so much more. I missed you, as if half of me had been torn away, and I was left with an aching wound which refused to heal.'

'Oh, I know,' she whispered in a ragged voice. 'I refused to admit it, but at night I used to dream of you.' She looked up, eyes smoky with remembrance. 'And I told myself that a woman always remembers her first lover—that old cliché, clinging to it as if it was a lifeline because I didn't dare face the truth. If Greg was out of my sphere as he obviously thought he was then you were as far out of reach as a star. Only I heard your voice in the shop,'—she began to smile without amusement—'I only heard your damned *voice*, I didn't even see you, and I knew just how stupid I'd been. For better or worse when you took me that night you took all of me, not just my body but my heart, you got inside my head, you made yourself a part of me.'

She stared at him with great accusing eyes, her mouth trembling, then suddenly burrowed her head into his chest, her arms twined tightly about him and wept as if her heart would break.

'Darling,' he whispered, when she lay spent and quiet against him, 'oh, darling, can't you see it's the same for me too? Why else did I inveigle my way in to your father's house, make love to you without shame and remorse when I knew you didn't want it? God knows, I've always prided myself on my honesty; you've come ominously close to making me forget all my principles. If my experience worries you I'm sorry for the other women there have been in my life, but won't you believe that from now on there's only room for you?'

Christabel sighed, exhausted yet clear-minded as she had not been for months. 'Yes, of course,' she said simply. 'I'm not even jealous of those other women.' One slender hand smoothed a path through the damp tangle of hair her tears had matted. 'Just remember that if you ever look at anyone else I'll kill her. And then you. And then,' she finished gloomily, 'probably myself.'

He chuckled. 'I'll remember,' he promised, half-serious as her threat had been. 'In the meantime, don't you think we'd better get up? I don't know what time Donald and Elaine are due back, but I for one don't relish trying to explain to Scott why you and I are in bed together without clothes on and it's not even bedtime.'

She smiled, still unsure of him. Although he had said that he was in love with her he had meant I want, I need, I must have you, but what she felt for him far transcended the hungry words, the words of desire and passion and selfishness.

'I know,' he said, surprising her with his quick comprehension once again. 'However, we can't talk now. Get dressed, and we'll do it then.'

But after they had showered and changed into dry clothes she was shy again, and he a stranger.

'Would you like a cup of coffee?' she asked in stilted tones.

'I think it would be a good idea.' He smiled rather ironically at her quick retreat and when she carried the tray back into the room he was standing by the window, silhouetted against the greyness outside, a big, lean, hard man wrapped in a cloak of self-command that seemed impervious.

Her hands shook as she poured. She looked swiftly up to see if he had noticed, but he was still staring out of the window, the autocratic, beautiful profile unmoved.

Oh, how she loved him! Within her breast her heart moved and she got to her feet and gave Alex his coffee, the rosy colour his lovemaking had caused fading into pallor.

They spoke little while they drank and that little commonplaces, then Alex rang the hospital and confirmed that the man they had rescued was safe and well enough to be discharged.

When he came back into the room Christabel had re-lit the fire and was sitting on her haunches beside it, staring into the flames. She lifted her eyes and watched him warily, the barriers firmly back in place.

He smiled and she asked numbly, not knowing how to lead up to the question in any other way, 'Why did you ask me to be your mistress?'

He made a muffled sound deep in his throat but didn't touch her—and oh, she needed the reassurance of his touch just then. After a moment he said 'I wanted to hurt you. You'd just rejected me—totally, completely. We'd made love and it was magical, a kind of physical communion, like nothing I'd ever experienced before. Until then I'd begun to think—to hope almost—that the first time was just a freak, a one-in-a-million combination of circumstances; perhaps the much-vaunted pleasure of initiating a virgin.' Some of the cynicism Christabel hated showed for a moment in his face and voice and she made a nervous gesture, turning her face away so that he couldn't see the hurt his words caused.

'No, listen,' he insisted. 'It wasn't that. I knew you were something special, but God knows, I was too hardened to believe in love, especially at first sight. I thought—I was knocked off my feet that second time, totally at a loss, and too wary, God forgive me, to appreciate what I'd found. But I knew that I couldn't let it slip through my fingers. I suggested that we keep in touch——' He broke off and came across to where she sat, slender shoulders slightly hunched, head downbent.

'Don't look so—so defeated, Christabel, or I'll have to take you in my arms and comfort you and once I do that you know what will happen, don't you,' he threatened softly.

Colour flooded her face and throat. She looked up, met the leashed passion of his expression with an answering hunger. And Alex swung on his heel and walked back to the window.

'Alex.'

'Just keep your head lowered,' he advised with hard humour, 'because when you look at me I find it very difficult to think, let alone be rational. And we'd better be rational, even if it's only for a few minutes.'

He stood for a moment as though searching for

words while Christabel watched him, hands laced together so tightly in her lap that the fingers were bloodless. Whatever Alex had to say to her was of vital importance, yet she was impatient for him to be finished so that they could lose themselves in their heated, silent world of passion.

'You're not helping much,' he said wryly. 'That's been half the trouble. You hated yourself for responding to me with such ardour and I, like a fool, thought that whatever was between us was purely physical.'

'Purely?'

He smiled. 'Impurely, then. Every time we tried to get closer to each other this—this overmastering desire got in the way. That first night, you were hurt and angry at Greg for jilting you. I realised that it was pain and pride which made you behave so forwardly.'

She nodded. 'Yes. He had plans, you know. I was to be his mistress.' She listened to the swift harsh oath without flinching. 'I—well, I thought I was in love with him. I had to run because I didn't think I could resist him for much longer. At Sarah's wedding he was with your sister and I had to show him and everyone else that I didn't care, that I was capable of catching a much bigger fish.' She lifted her eyes, her voice deepening suddenly as she added with a twisted smile, 'I would love you even if we'd never met again for being there and salving my pride so superbly. Greg was furious!'

'I know.' Alex hadn't moved, but he suddenly seemed much farther away. 'I overheard your conversation.'

'I see. No wonder you thought I was free for the taking!'

The broad shoulders lifted. 'No, I thought you were very gallant and I wanted you like I'd never wanted another woman before. I didn't realise you'd not slept with anyone. When I did I was totally astounded. And I shocked myself by being pleased.'

'Whereas I thought there was something wrong with

me,' Christabel said in a low voice. 'I was supposed to be in love with Greg, yet I'd made love with you and it was mind-blowing. The next morning I couldn't leave Brisbane fast enough. I couldn't even blame it on the champagne. I didn't have any sign of a hangover.'

Silence, then she went on, 'Like the man said, just a crazy mixed-up kid. Then you came here and you were—different, somehow—oh, you teased and you mocked, but you seemed gentler, and although I told myself I'd forgotten you it all came back. I wanted you every time I looked at you, but for a while there I thought I was falling in love with you too.'

'Until the plans for Rangitatau broke.' Alex leaned out of the window, scanning the sea, frowning, the lean torso perfectly balanced against the grey light outside. 'And then you hated me.'

'A little. When we made love again you—you asked me to live with you. And I hated you much more for that.'

He sounded strained, the deep confident voice hesitating, choosing his words with care. 'Because you made it quite clear that for you the whole sex bit was just a temporary aberration, something you despised yourself for. I didn't know—I thought what we had was rare and precious enough to be cherished, even though I didn't realise that I loved you.'

He paused and when she said nothing asked quietly, 'Have you any idea how it feels to have a gift thrown back in your face, Christabel?'

'I thought that was what you did to me.'

'I know.' As another gust of wind hit the glass he turned and looked across at her, slender shoulders held back as she watched the flames. 'As I said before, my darling, the physical magic between us made it difficult for both of us to see past it to the really important things—the fact that we have many tastes in common, that we share the same sense of humour, that we can talk for hours and never bore each other. I should have known, because I'm the more experienced—I think, subconsciously, I did know. That's why I was so cruel to you.'

At last he turned and came towards her, pulling her up into his warm arms.

'We fell in love,' he said into her hair, holding her loosely yet without any possibility of escape. 'We should have known that only love could give us the power to hurt each other so badly. I went back home to forget you and I tried—God, how I tried! And I was lonely.'

'Oh, I know,' she said shakenly, lifting her head to press her face into the warm strength of his neck. 'Always lonely, always hoping and yet knowing that there was no hope.'

Beneath her lips the pulse at his throat beat heavily, the fine skin throbbing above it. She turned her head and pressed kisses downwards to the open neck of his shirt while one of her hands came up to curve around the back of his neck.

'No,' he said in a thickened voice, pulling her chin up. 'Not yet, darling heart, my sweet wanton. Are you going to marry me?'

'You know I am.'

Alex laughed, the sound oddly distorted through the walls of his chest. 'I only know that I'm not going away without you. If I had to shackle you to me, I was going to do it, even if it meant making you pregnant and forcing you to marry me that way.'

'When did you decide that?'

'Before I came back, this last time.'

Christabel stared up at him, astounded and not entirely believing him. 'But—you were a swine when you came back.'

'Mmm.' The dark features hardened into anger. 'Because the first thing I saw was you and that bloody vet, tastefully arranged in what appeared to be a passionate clinch. I damned near burst a blood vessel trying to control myself.' He shook her, not gently, no longer showing the icy restraint she remembered from that incident. 'I think poor Donald wondered if he was going to have bloodshed on his land,' he finished harshly.

'Dad?'

'Yes. He saw my face.' He gave a short bark of laughter totally without humour. 'You know your father! He said "Steady on there, boy", and it was only my hope that you were doing to me what you'd done to Greg that stopped me from dismembering bloody Nate!'

'Oh, you were right. You read me so well. I'd heard you and Dad talking and I couldn't bear it. . . .' Gentle fingers, not entirely steady, touched his implacable face, tracing the cruel sensual line of his lips. 'Poor Nate must have wondered what on earth was going on. Afterwards I felt guilty about using him, but I'd had enough pain. I wanted to make you disgusted with me so that you'd leave me alone because. . . .' Christabel's voice trailed away as colour rushed into her cheeks. Alex had just, very gently, bitten the tip of her finger, but at her sudden embarrassment he looked down with leaping, glinting lights of laughter in his eyes.

'Because?' he prompted.

'Because I knew you only had to crook your little finger and I'd come running.' She lifted a gaze in which some of her torment still showed, turbulent and darkened. 'I felt cheap and—and *swamped* by you. I was an addict, I thought I hated you and yet I was—am—totally hooked. I've always been shameless where you're concerned. Abandoned and wicked and totally without shame and it's not *me*. I thought I loved Greg, yet I'd kept him at bay without too much pain. But you, whom I didn't even *know*, I couldn't resist.'

He laughed and kissed her, fast and hard, then lifted his head. 'Just the way you should be,' he said with immense satisfaction.

'Listen, is that the car?'

'Yes. Ready to face them?'

Colour washed her face again and she looked shyly into his face, fitting her hand against the strong curve of his cheek· as her eyes held his, her love and need transfiguring her so that she was radiant, warm and glowing and vital.

'Well, Donald will be relieved,' he said, his gaze kindling as it swept her face.

'Did he guess?'

'I can be conventional when the occasion calls for it. I'd just finished asking him for your hand when we opened the door on to that touching embrace.'

Christabel laughed suddenly. 'Sly old Dad,' she said, and Alex laughed with her, then handfasted, joined in laughter and passion and a deep tenderness, together as they would always be from now on, they went out to meet the rest of the family.

Harlequin Plus

A WORD ABOUT THE AUTHOR

Robyn Donald cannot remember ever being unable to read. She learned the skill at a very early age; and today, she claims, reading remains one of her great pleasures, "if not a vice."

Robyn, her husband and their two children make their home in a small country village in the historic Bay of Islands in the far north of New Zealand. Both the climate and the people are friendly, and her family enjoys sailing in particular and the outdoor life in general.

Her other interests include cooking, music and astronomy. And she finds history and archaeology especially fascinating because "they are about the sum total of human experience."

When she writes, Robyn visualizes scenes that she knows and loves. The actual germ of a story arrives "ready-made from some recess of my brain, but," she adds, "it takes quite a while to work out the details!"

Yours FREE, with a home subscription to SUPERROMANCE™

Now you never have to miss reading the newest **SUPERROMANCES**... because they'll be delivered right to your door.

Start with your **FREE** LOVE BEYOND DESIRE. You'll be enthralled by this powerful love story...from the moment Robin meets the dark, handsome Carlos and finds herself involved in the jealousies, bitterness and secret passions of the Lopez family. Where her own forbidden love threatens to shatter her life.

Your **FREE** LOVE BEYOND DESIRE is only the beginning. A subscription to **SUPERROMANCE** lets you look forward to a long love affair. Month after month, you'll receive four love stories of heroic dimension. Novels that will involve you in spellbinding intrigue, forbidden love and fiery passions.

You'll begin this series of sensuous, exciting contemporary novels...written by some of the top romance novelists of the day...with four every month.

And this big value...each novel, almost 400 pages of compelling reading...is yours for only $2.50 a book. Hours of entertainment every month for so little. Far less than a first-run movie or pay-TV. Newly published novels, with beautifully illustrated covers, filled with page after page of delicious escape into a world of romantic love...delivered right to your home.